The Windows to a Shapeshifter's Soul

Booker G. A. Feniks

The Whumpy Printing Press

Cover Design by Nicole Alessi

Cover Illustration by Hen Towers

I dedicate this book to my family, and to my grandmother who never got to see me grow into the man I am today, but without whom I never would have gotten where I am today.

And I dedicate it to myself because, through it all, I always stayed true to who I was, and if I can't be proud of what I have accomplished, no one else will.

CONTENTS

— · —

CONTENT WARNINGS

This story contains the following content:
- Captivity

- Restraints

- Dehumanisation

- Torture

- Character Death

- Death of parents

If this book isn't for you, no worries! But if it is, we hope you enjoy this story about a magizoologist and his new job ...

1

Josef, Brooke, and Vanja

He felt their eyes watching him, multiple pairs that bored into the back of his head. Tracing his steps through the apartment, homing in on him wherever he turned. He moved with slow, languid steps, weaving between piles of discarded books and haphazardly placed furniture. All the while they watched him, those piercing eyes. Following him, moving through the empty space he left behind him, silent footsteps echoing in his mind.

Then she pounced, and Josef crashed to the ground with a resounding laugh. His cackle joined the excited yipping of his three-headed dog. His small, rustic apartment was filled with the sounds of their combined joy.

"Spot, Spot!" He pushed at the three great maws yawning over him, dripping hot saliva onto his freshly pressed shirt. The central head, with its little pink bowtie, whined and pushed at Josef's arms, trying to smoosh itself under his hands. The left head, with a bright red bow snuggled between its ears, was snuffling at the side of Josef's head, drooling incessantly in its excitement. The right head, with a purple bow attached to its right ear, was licking her master's face, while her tail was trailing a streak of fire through the air as it wagged and wagged.

"Stop it," Josef breathed out, trying to grab some air. "You'll set off the fire alarm again, silly pup." With a great push and many whines, he managed to dislodge Spot, trying to pet all three heads at once with only his two human hands. She was bouncing around him, barking in three deep, baritone voices, her coal-black fur soft under his touch.

"I was just getting you your food," Josef admonished her, pressing his finger against the warm, wet nose of the central head. Her coarse tongue darted out and almost swallowed his entire wrist whole, leaving hot slobber to cool on his shirt cuff. The glasses he lost in the kerfuffle he found under the coffee table. He gave the dark lenses a cursory dust-off and inspected the thin, metallic frames. They sat securely atop his crooked nose, hand-made specifically for his face, hiding from the world his russet eyes. Without the second set of eyelids his full-blooded dragon kin had, he found the world painfully bright, and his eyes were sensitive to almost everything. His apartment stayed dark, with dimmed lights and pulled-down curtains. Luckily, Spot was also used to the darkness, still dancing around his legs, rubbing her thick body against his abdomen. He could only hope the fur wouldn't show on his black slacks.

He set about feeding Spot her morning portion of hot coals and bison flank. She had three bowls made of iron, decorated with little coloured symbols corresponding to each head. Whenever Josef slept in late, she would grab all three bowls and jump on him, hanging them over his head as he tried to rub the sleep from his eyes. She loved those bowls, handcrafted just for her, the way they clanked and thunked. It was the very first thing his uncle taught him about cerberi: they had sensitive hearing, and they loved sound-based toys.

There was a picture on the mantelpiece, right above Spot's bowls, that featured his uncles. Brooke Ryan and Josef Braun were a handsome pair: a six feet, two inches, hairy, Irish black-smith, and a five feet, six inches, nerdy, German dog trainer. They met through his mother, Brooke's long-suffering twin sister.

Uncle Josef had been the most famous magizoologist of his generation and the owner of an award-winning show cerberus. It was on Josef's own birthday that his uncle gifted him Spot II, the descendant of a long line of show dogs. Alongside her came the three metal bowls, Uncle Brooke having worked on them for weeks. Josef still remembered the way his uncles stood together, arms around each other's waists, heads pressed against one another. His mother had called it love at first sight, love until the very end. Watching them stand over him, Spot in his arms, they looked like the happiest pair of people in the world. Josef had felt honoured when he was asked to help design their gravestone. Love like that only comes once in a lifetime.

Spot bumped against his legs, her bowls already empty, pulling Josef out of his reverie.

"Shit, I'm gonna be late!"

In record time he had run a brush through his curly, auburn hair, dug out his house keys from the deepest recesses of his couch, and left the house in a dress shirt still covered in drying cerberus slobber. *I'm so not getting this job.*

2

---·---

THE FACILITY FOR THE CONSERVATION OF MAGICAL CREATURES

The Facility for the Conservation of Magical Creatures (known as the FCMC amongst the common rabble) loomed above Josef like an omen. The Behemoth of dark metal glinted in the morning sunlight, its many windowed eyes staring down at the man approaching it. The massive double doors were an unwelcome invitation into the belly of a beast that burrowed deep beneath the earth. The weaving tails of corridors and hallways that stretched beneath the small city were only rumours, but each rumour held a grain of truth within it. The corporate, metal Behemoth was just a taste of the beast that was the FCMC, and Josef willingly approached it. He felt like a knight of old approaching a dragon, in the days where people still thought of dragons as mindless, brutish beasts. He felt like Sir Thaddeus the Dragon Friend, the first man to ever study his scaled foes. The very man who brought the world of humans out of a dark, deadly, terrified age, into the age of enlightenment and knowledge.

Sir Thaddeus' face was plastered upon a plate made of gold hanging above the double doors of the entrance. His handsome, almost kingly profile was turned towards the profile of another man, his expression severe. The smiling, handsome face of Charles Young contrasted with the stern face of his ancestor, both of them framing a ring of black metal inserted into the golden plate. Both grandfather and grandson, the first man to study a dragon and the man behind the genius of the FCMC, stared at the curling body of a snake biting its own tail.

Every time Josef looked at the old logo of Limbo Laboratories, he couldn't help but shiver. Why anyone would incorporate the symbol of such an organisation, old and dead as it was, into their own signage was beyond him. How much they differed, with the FCMC striving for the protection of all magical beings. The Limbo Labs, meanwhile, were better off forgotten in the annals of history.

Josef walked through the double doors of the FCMC building. He pushed his glasses further up his crooked nose and ran a hand through his curly hair once more. He caught a glimpse of himself in the reflection of a bell at the welcome desk. His dark, olive skin stood out against the bright blue dress shirt he wore. His skin-toned lips were turning red from where he was worrying away at them with his teeth, picking at the dry skin there until he could faintly taste his own blood. His cheeks were pleasantly round, but he noticed that his collarbones stuck out too much. His mother's funeral, he realised for the first time in weeks, had taken far more out of him than he had anticipated. He supposed that he'd needed to see the effect for himself to believe it, despite all the times his sister Vanja and his father pointed it out to him.

Out of the corner of his eye he saw the glint of metal, and he focused his attention on a statue placed in the centre of the room. The tall, looming presence of Sir Thaddeus was much more appealing than his own visage, with its broad shoulders and thick chest. It was mounted upon a base bearing a plaque with his name and was held up securely by the steel cords attached to its back.

"Can I help you?" The receptionist appeared behind the welcome desk before he so much as leant towards the bell. Maybe just looking at it was enough to summon the clearly bored, possibly underpaid young woman with a drawling, accented voice. She scratched the corner of her red lips with an equally red, manicured nail, and the motion made her very shiny, very golden hoop earrings swing. Josef wasn't sure what was more glaring about her: the almost eye-bleeding shade of red that she seemed to prefer or the far-too-overgrown horns growing out of her head. He didn't even think to mention the horns; he doubted that she didn't know. Still, poor girl, had the money for a manicure but couldn't even find a good buccicure place in town.

"I'm here for a job appointment." He coughed, fumbling with his wallet and managing to not drop his ID when giving it to the receptionist. She didn't take it, didn't even move her plump hand away from her mouth, just took a cursory glance at the thin, plastic rectangle, and then looked back at him.

"Right, nephew of the hellhound trainer, yes?" She quirked her red lip up into something that almost resembled a smile, and Josef wondered if Vanja, if she were there with him, would like her.

Then he realised what she had said and felt his cheeks flush hotly. "I, uh ... "

"It's your name; it gives you away." She giggled, and it sounded melodic, almost tempting. "Not that it's not a nice name, but certainly not very common. Not the whole combination, at least." She added the last sentence after a moment of silence, in which Josef tried his best not to choke on his quickening breaths. He pushed his glasses further up his nose, bunching up the fabric of his slacks with his fist.

"Nice eyes, though. Got a dragon in your family?"

He swallowed and let out a breath. "Yes, actually. Adopted great-grandfather, passed on his genes through the paternal line."

"Explains the lack of wings," she added, her grin only growing wider. "I'm a satyr, hence the horns. Full-blooded, but most people don't really get to see the hooves."

She didn't seem to mind his little snort or his shy smile. "Always nice to meet someone else with non-human ancestry. We seem to gravitate to each other, almost."

"It is nice, isn't it? You'd think we'd be more widespread by now, what with it being the twenty-first century. You know, with the internet and all." She sent him a wink, and he realised that her eyeshadow was of a similar shade of red as her lips and nails. "That why you're interested in working with magical creatures?"

His smile became more earnest. He could feel his eyes crinkle at the edges, slightly lifting up his glasses. "No, actually. You see, I originally wanted to be an athlete like my mother, but right before her death she told me I didn't need to be like her to make her proud and ... "

"Uhu ... " She breathed out slowly, giving him a look he couldn't quite place. He held his breath for a moment, looking at her through the dark lenses of his glasses, fiddling with a stray thread from his trousers.

"My sister gave me the idea, inspired by my uncle. The hell-hound trainer one," he eventually said, breathing out each word slowly and deliberately. She gave him a nod, no longer smiling at him, no longer softly gazing at him with slightly closed eyelids, a finger pressing gently against the corner of her lip.

"Well." She coughed, looking back to her computer. "Hate for you to be late, talking to me like that. I'll let the guide know you're here."

"The guide?"

When she looked back up at him, it was with a blank look. "The tour guide."

"I'm sorry, I came here for a job interview."

"No." She kept staring at him. "You have an appointment."

"Where does a tour factor into this?"

"You'll be joining four other interviewees. You'll be touring around the facility, being introduced to the magical creatures you'll be working with." She paused, and when Josef didn't respond, she continued, "It's how Mr Young wants it done. He wants hands-on interviews, not just a conversation behind a desk." She turned back to her computer, her blank stare unwavering but her head swivelling downwards and to the side. Josef rubbed at his temple, trying to make sense of it. He felt as if he was going mad, as if this were something he obviously should have known.

Vanja and he had done research. It was true that the job searching website had mentioned a 'job appointment' as opposed to a 'job interview', but Josef had assumed this was a mistyping, an intern who made a mistake, nothing to focus on, not really.

The receptionist with the red ... everything waved him over to the elevator and told him which button he was supposed to press. His stomach clenched when the elevator jerked and began moving, and he wasn't sure if it was just the locomotion or if he was making one big mistake.

3

GALAXIES IN YOUR EYES

He arrived at a room with five other people already waiting for him. He went to open his mouth, bumble out an apology, but he was silenced by a sharp-looking woman sitting at the head of a meeting table. She waved him into a seat next to a man, about his own age, with a blue tie and a diamond earring. The only thing Josef could think about as he sat down next to him was just how much those two accessories clashed.

"As I was saying," the woman at the front said with a voice like the beginning of an earthquake, and a severe expression that terrified Josef, "here at the Facility we value hands-on work above all else. In your job working with the endangered animals we keep at the Facility, you will come in contact with beasts that you won't find in a regular zoo. Many of them are dangerous; some of them are even deadly. Very few of them are peaceful or harmless, but even with such creatures you must ensure that you act accordingly. That is why the Facility does not conduct regular interviews. All of you already possess knowledge of, and even experience with, working with magical creatures of some kind. The thing that will set apart those who will and those who won't get the job is the ability to adapt and make split-second decisions. We need to ensure that you are prepared to work with the creatures entrusted to us, and today you will do so in a contained environment. If you do well here, you may look forward to further training and a bright future in the conservation of magical creatures. Now, are we ready to head down to the veterinary level?"

All four of the people around the table nodded, and Josef followed suit only a few seconds later.

During the tour guide's lengthy speech, he had a good chance to look at who he was competing with. Out of the four, the person he sat beside was the only other man in the group. The other three interviewees were women, one also his age, another that looked barely out of college, and one who looked older than his mother.

The youngest, although looking to be barely eighteen, must have had relevant experience, meaning she was most likely very confident in her skills. She was dressed in a pink skirt and a black shirt that reminded him of something one of Vanja's exes would wear, with pentagram earrings reminding him of a completely different ex.

The oldest woman had silver shot through her blonde hair and wrinkles in the corners of her eyes. Out of them all, he expected her to be the most likely to get a job. With her age came experience, and Josef could only imagine what sort of experience this woman had.

The last woman, the one more his age, had freckles and wine-coloured hands. The scales that travelled from her fingertips to the edges of her wrists were striking in colour, and their particular pattern upon her palms made him think that she was a demon. And yet he was second-guessing himself. The work of a magizoologist required patience and focus, traits demons weren't known to possess. She had an ace up her sleeve, he could feel it.

The fourth person in the room, the man with the diamond earring, was handsome, even despite the blue tie. He had scars all across his fingers and his wrists that stood out starkly against his dark skin, and Josef could immediately tell he was a former mage vet's apprentice. The scar over his right pinkie was shaped like a baby cockatrice beak, and the burn across his left wrist was most likely the work of an egg-bound phoenix.

I'm not getting this job, Josef thought to himself again.

***

He felt their eyes on him, countless gazes boring into him, watching from behind thin bars. They trailed after him as he meandered between the medical equipment strewn about the many emptied-out rooms. He was stuck at the back of the tour group, surprised that they weren't being introduced to any other vets or caretakers.

Up ahead, the tour guide was talking in short, clipped sentences, things Josef couldn't quite catch. He knew one thing: no one was allowed to touch anything, not until they were authorised. Later on, they were each supposed to be assigned a creature, something small and harmless like a golden goose or a rainbow fish. They were supposed to show their knowledge of handling magical creatures, but Josef wasn't thrilled about it. He would have preferred a basilisk or maybe a sprite but knew he would probably end up explaining to the tour guide the science behind jackalope fur resembling that of a common deer.

He was also told not to pay too much attention to any of the animals around him. Many of them were shy and got nervous when people looked at them. From the brief glimpses he allowed himself, he found a veritable menagerie. All the animals were in cages of different shapes and sizes. They had blankets and food bowls, plastic water bottles hanging off the thin bars. Some had IVs, others wore visible bandages, while most just seemed lethargic or tired. Josef felt his heart hurt at the sight of them. He noticed a larger cage with a sickly-looking unicorn without its horn, and he had to bite down on his knuckle to keep from crying. In another corner he found himself enamoured by a three-headed viper bearing the scars of a fight upon its glistening, scaled body.

Then there was the kitten. A small, black, thin kitten. It was in an impossibly tiny cage on wheels, being moved by three different scientists. They carried it past adolescent draconids, a tank holding a kelpie, and a giant, monstrous wolf the size of a car. Its black, bottomless eyes managed to catch his gaze, unblinking as it scrutinised him. Josef felt a chill run down his spine, a hand jumping to his throat where he was struggling to swallow. The tiny kitten wore a tiny muzzle that linked to a chain attached to the top of the cage. The chain was long enough to let it lay down but not long enough to let it walk to the edges of the cage. It scratched at the floor with mindless abandon, staring at Josef all the while. It was as if he couldn't look away, as if he was being hypnotised. This was a creature he didn't recognise, and yet he felt as if he knew it. Inwardly, in another plane of existence, he knew it, but the words weren't there to describe it.

"Mr Ryan."

Josef bit down on his tongue, swivelling around to the rest of the group. The tour guide was looking at him, her mouth forming a thin line and her eyebrows downturned.

"Yes?"

"I would be very happy if you stayed with the group," she hissed through clenched teeth, "and didn't look at the creatures like I had asked you to. Especially not in the Dangerous section."

Josef gulped and nodded, hanging his head and returning to his spot at the end of the line. He looked back, and the scientists carrying that thing were already gone. As he walked, listening to the droning words of the tour guide, he couldn't get his mind off it. The chain, the muzzle, the eyes. The little tag at the bottom of the cage read Subject-20-465 and nothing else. No species, no age, nothing that he noticed on all the other animals. And those eyes.

As the group turned the corner, Josef looked up and saw a corridor lined with doors, each one with a name plaque at the top beneath a small window. These were offices, and as Josef walked past one, he saw a poster hanging up on the other side of the little window. The poster was of a pink and blue nebula against a black and starry background, and it was in that moment that Josef knew.

The kitten had eyes that reflected the stars.

4

EXPECTATIONS AND FIREBIRDS

"Brooke, come sit!" Vanja's lilting voice brought Josef out of his thoughts, her pale face lit up and her slender arm pointing to the seat beside her. Her long, black hair was put up into an elaborate braid she had, very likely, done herself, and her dark blue lipstick was perfectly contrasted with her pale greenish-blue eyes. She had a slight accent as she spoke, trilling out her Rs in a way that Josef always liked the sound of. It was as if she was purring every time she called him Brooke.

Jozić Vanja had been a Croatian painter in her youth. By 'youth', she really meant that she had won a few art competitions at school at the age of five. In actuality, she was his adopted younger sister, Spot's favourite person in all the world, and the daughter his father, Dante, had always wanted. She spoiled the three-headed pup, and Josef never knew where she got all the money to buy her so many treats. Josef thought she never paid rent and sold her art online to fancy art critics for way more than it was worth. And she had enough free time on her hands to find him a job. Uncle Josef would've been proud.

"We've been coming to Déjà Brew a lot lately. Who caught your eye this time, Rus?" The smell of fresh coffee wafted out of the door to the quaint coffee shop they sat outside of. A few tables down from them, a teenage couple was making googly eyes at each other, holding hands atop the little plastic tables that looked like they had been carved out of wood, legs and all.

"New cashier fell into my eye. He's so cute, breath of fresh air after my ex." She giggled as she sipped her decaf, trailing a long, black nail over the edge of the coffee cup. She was wearing a low-cut, black dress and cord bracelets. Her earrings were the most casual thing about her, plain silver studs.

"So, he emo or goth?"

"Goth!" Vanja squealed, squeezing her fists and shaking them in excitement. "I waited to bring out my goth clothes since Julia moved back to Poland."

Josef nodded, picking up the foam cup Vanja bought for him before he got there. "He from around here, then?" He pushed his glasses further up his nose, then traced his eyes over the scene inside the café. He didn't see any cashier that looked even remotely goth.

"I don't know. Yet! I will find out, you just watch. But enough about me, how did job interview go!"

The coffee suddenly became too bitter for him, and he had to set it back down with a pronounced grimace. "Doubt I'll get it." He swiped at his mouth with the back of his hand, and let his glasses slide down his nose to look Vanja right in her black-rimmed eyes. "Although I doubt any of us will get the job."

"Why? What happen?"

"Oh, I let my curiosity get the better of me and broke the rule of not looking at the creatures." When Vanja gave him a blank look, he cleared his throat. The next five minutes were taken up with him explaining, in detail, exactly what he knew about the weird interview structure at the FCMC.

"Make sense, yes."

Josef hadn't touched his coffee since he began explaining, but in that moment, he didn't need it to choke. "They could have at least told us in advance! I wore my best shirt for this interview."

"It have Spot slobber on it, can't be best shirt. One of best shirts, I would understand, but not best shirt." Vanja took a sip of her drink, staring down at him over the rim of her cup. The little shrug she did had Josef's blood pressure rising.

"Will you let me finish explaining?"

"Go ahead." And then she smiled, and he could no longer make himself feel mad.

He cleared his throat once more, took another sip of his coffee, and carried on, "Well, we eventually ended up in a medical room. I was on thin ice already at that point, and I didn't have high hopes for what was to come. We were to go alphabetically, however, and I ended up being last, so I had the chance to see how well the other four people did. The handsome guy with the diamond earring was given a jackalope to handle. Turns out, he knew absolutely nothing about non-avian monsters, and I had to show him how to hold the poor bunny. The tour guide recommended that he go work for a magical aviary instead."

Vanja let out a twinkling giggle, and her eyes went blank for a few seconds. *Artists.* Josef shook his head. She always drifted off when thinking too deeply.

Then, when she came back to the world of the living, she ripped a small notebook out of her purse and began sketching in it. Josef gave her a few moments to get her thoughts out onto the paper before he carried on with his story. With each tale he had to give her a pause, time to commit her imagination to a physical form, before he could move on again.

"The one that reminded me of your exes ... "

"Pink skirt and pentagram earrings."

"Yes, thank you. She looked the youngest but turned out to be older than the rest of us combined."

"Ooooh, really?" Vanja's eyes were twinkling as she looked at him. Her elbows were firmly stuck to the table, and her chin rested in her open palms.

"Yes, she's actually a fairy. Out of the five of us, she's the most likely to get the job. Well, maybe. Fairies, or fae-folk, are beings of pure magic, and the most sentient of the fae species, and the only ones able to take on a human size and shape. They don't get along well with other fae species."

"What did she get?"

"A brownie."

"What?"

"Remember when I told you about the domovoy?"

"Oh! Little house helpers!"

"Yes. I had to calm it down for her, because the two kept on screaming at each other in the fae tongue." At the reminder of that he reached up to massage the bridge of his nose. His migraine was returning, and he doubted it would leave anytime soon.

"We live in nation of UK, does FCMC get many fae?"

"Too many for a fairy to comfortably work for them."

"Tell me of demon lady next."

"Yes, well. As I told you previously, demons are known for their impulsiveness, like fairies are known for their egos, humans for their competitiveness, dragons for their greed, h—...
"

"Lecture me later, carry on with story, Brooke." She gave him a pout and her lips looked like a blueberry. Over her shoulder, Josef saw the young couple standing up and leaving. He didn't even notice how he was forlornly looking after them, until Vanja was snapping her fingers before his eyes.

"Sorry, right. Ahem." He slipped his glasses off his nose before continuing, "The demon lady, I think you would have liked her. She wasn't impulsive at all, and actually was the calmest of us all, I think. Her downfall was her, well ... her hydrophobia."

22

"Her ... fear of water?"

"Yes. I know, an elemental creature, sort of weird to have a fear of one of the elements. But humans can have mechanophobia and we're the ones that make the robots, so anything is possible, really. Anyway, they gave her a hippocampus. She burst into tears."

"Poor dear. You know I am half rusałka, I adore water. Is perfectly safe, really." She flashed him her pointed teeth, and he bared his own fangs back at her. His weren't nearly as noticeable or impressive, but the burst of smoke from his nose easily did the trick.

"That's why phobias are irrational fears, Rus," he explained over Vanja's laughter. "She was so scared, I had to come over to help her calm down. You know how I always carry a coal in my pocket for Spot, so I gave it to her to fiddle with and she really ended up liking setting it on fire and extinguishing it. I even let her keep it."

"Aww. You're sunshine, Brooke. What about last person?"

"Ah, the woman who seemed older than my mother. She was another human, like the diamond earring guy. I thought she would have gotten the job; I was so sure. Someone who has lived that long surely would have a lot of experience."

"What happened then?"

"Well, she was given a baku."

"Cute dream eaters with little elephant trunks."

"Yes, the one you drew me a picture of for my twenty-ninth birthday. It had eaten a dream that didn't sit right with it and needed help expelling it. The woman didn't ... she didn't know how that works."

"Let me guess: she thought baku give her bad dreams?" She had that cheeky smile on her face again. Those rusałka genes came out the strongest when she smiled. Her pale, blueish gums were pulled back to further elongate her sharp, pointed teeth. Her light greenish eyes were the colour of the moss that grew along the riverbanks, and they crinkled at the edges when she grinned.

Josef took another sip of his coffee and hummed thoughtfully, messing around with his glasses, moving them from one side of the table to the other. "Mhm, which isn't at all how these creatures function, after all. They only eat dreams, and they especially like eating nightmares to help people. They don't give people nightmares."

"So, she didn't understand basic of how baku even work?" Vanja was sounding gleeful now, replacing her chin atop the little bridge she made with her intertwined fingers, her bony elbows resting atop the table.

"No, and that was when we found out that she applied for the wrong job." Josef's eyes flitted between Vanja and the waiter who had exited the café while they talked, hands full of packed trays and a pleasant smile on his tanned, bearded face. "She wanted to apply for a secretary job, but something went wrong, there was a glitch in the system. I ended up helping the baku instead."

"Aw, poor dear. Did she get transferred?"

The waiter dropped the trays off at the only other taken table, before a skeletal young woman. "The tour guide said she would talk to HR about it, but that the woman shouldn't count on getting an interview. She had multiple chances to correct the mistake and didn't take them." Josef watched out of the corner of his eye as the woman unhinged her jaws to a ridiculous degree, before swallowing the food presented to her right before the waiter. It took her only a few seconds, and once she was done her skin was flushed, and she had gained a healthy chubbiness to her cheeks. She gave the waiter a pleasant smile, and he gave her a knowing one back, before picking the trays up. However interesting the snake demon was, it was the waiter, as he was leaving, that held onto Josef's attention. The leg braces he wore over his work boots were shiny, and his eyes were a pleasant shade of purple.

"True, true. Oh, but Brooke! How did you do!" Vanja's yell brought him back to his own table and back to his long-since-cold coffee.

"I was given a raróg."

Vanja's eyes began to shine. "Song raróg or flame raróg?"

"Song raróg, the small ones. I don't think they would have let us handle a fire bird at this stage, even a docile one."

25

"But they let you handle hippocampus!" Her smile turned into a pouty grimace again, and she crossed her arms over her chest.

"Yes, but hippocampi, like the rest of their horse-hybrid cousins, such as the unicorn or the pegasus, have a higher intelligence level than most species of fire birds. They are less unpredictable than a bird that can literally set itself on fire."

"True, I suppose."

"But yes, they had me deal with a raróg. The poor thing had lost its voice and couldn't bring happiness to people anymore. Turns out that it had, quite literally, lost its voice on the wind while flying. The tour guide took the li'l guy back from me and passed it on to an actual employee. I would have loved to go hunting for a raróg's voice, but that was the end of the interview."

Vanja had a thoughtful look on her face, her painted fingers gently massaging her pointed chin.

"Penny for your thoughts." Josef hummed, reaching his hand out teasingly to rest between them. Vanja grinned again, shooting him a wink.

"You're so silly, Brooke," she laughed. "How could you not get hired? You're perfectly fit for it!"

Josef let out a huff and a puff of air that dislodged a lock of hair from his eyes. "Yes, but I already told you, I broke the rules before the interview even started. And I'm sure they get plenty of people applying for the job, they are the FCMC, after all."

That sweet, little pout was back on Vanja's face, and she wagged a slender finger right before Josef's nose. "Brooke, Brooke. You don't know people at all. You don't even know yourself. If I, Oh Great Vanja, tell you you're getting job, you'll get job. Trust me, Boo." Her fingers wrapped around his wrists, and she turned their hands so that Josef's were resting in hers, palms up to the sky. He had very little in him of a dragon, but the hard, almost scaled skin upon his palms was one of the very few traits he had from his great-grandfather.

"If you say so, Oh Great Vanja. I didn't know rusałkas could tell the future."

Vanja flashed her sharp teeth at him in a smile.

"Nothing like that, Boo. Just woman's intuition."

5

HOT-BLOODED

Josef's father, Dante Rubino, was a tall, powerful-looking man, the husband of the late, famous Olympian, Elspeth Ryan. He stood a head taller than his son, who was already above average for a human. Dante had far more of a dragon in him than Josef, with his scaled hands and his sharp teeth, his warm body and his muscular frame. He had olive skin darker than his son's, and dark brown hair that contrasted with Josef's Irish genes almost viscerally. His mother had the same red hair as Josef, and when Dante and Elspeth stood together they looked like a princess and her prince, but each pulled from a different fairytale. Josef, the perfect little mix of Irish and Italian genes, with a German first name and an accent like an Englishman, never really fit into the perfect little picture that his parents made. Not him, not the little black sheep. Or the little white dragon, as his father always said.

Dante never really healed after Elspeth's death; Josef could see that. He seemed depressed, he was shedding at an unhealthy rate, he was barely eating. And yet he was managing, somehow, to put on a brave face for his son. Dragons bonded for life; Josef knew he didn't have long left with his father.

"How are you managing, hatchling?" Dante's voice was always soft, gentle like a warm breeze in the summer. He always called Josef 'hatchling', even long after Josef became an adult. It was a dragon cultural term of endearment between a parent and a child, but it only ever reminded Josef of the fact that he was too human to really be a dragon. Not like Vanja or his father, not like the fairy and demon women from the interview. He was too far removed from it all.

"I'm good, dad. I'm job hunting still." Josef was drinking a coffee again. It was two weeks after his interview; they were at the same café he and Vanja went to, drinking the exact same coffee as last time. His father didn't really drink coffee. He preferred the tiny, bite-sized pastries instead.

"Do you need help?" Half of the pastry platter was long since forgotten, his father's appetite clearly leaving him already. "If you're struggling with rent, I could help."

Josef smiled at him and looked his father in the eye over the top of his glasses. His father had red eyes darker than his own, with the identical slits in the centre and the clear, second eyelids that Josef lacked. Unlike with Josef, people could tell that Dante was part dragon long before they looked him in the eyes.

"I'm fine, dad. I have a lot saved up from when I did weightlifting. And you know that Uncle Sef and Uncle Brooke left me almost everything." Josef saw the wobble of his father's lip, and he steeled himself for what was to come.

"Wouldn't you like the cottage, hatchling?"

"Dad, no. Uncle Brooke left that to you and mom, and mom left it to you. I'm fine in my apartment; Spot has enough space, Vanja is my neighbour, it's close to my dream job, and the queer club is right down the street from me."

Dante seemed dejected at that. His face fell, and Josef didn't know how to read that.

"If you're sure," he mumbled, picking at his pastries once more.

Josef took another sip, holding the warm cup between his calloused hands, focusing on all the little points alongside his fingers where he could feel the spikes of heat. "Are you sure you wouldn't just like me to move in with you?"

Josef's father shook his head. "No, hatchling. You have your own life here, you're right ... "

"Dad." Josef wanted to say more. He wasn't sure *what* exactly he wanted to say, but he wanted to say *something*. That was when his phone rang. The vibrations against his thigh made him jump, scrambling for the little, black rectangle.

"Yes? Hello?" Dante focused on his pastries again while Josef turned his head to face the other way. He cupped the phone against his ear.

"Is this Mr Joseph Brooke Ryan?" said the voice on the other end of the receiver. Josef cringed, swallowing thickly.

"Yes, can I help you?"

"I am calling on behalf of the Facility for the Conservation of Magical Creatures to let you know that you have been accepted into the role of a Junior Caretaker." The voice was prim and proper, soft and lightly high-pitched. It spoke so casually, so matter-of-factly, that Josef didn't fully comprehend what it said at first.

"Alright, thank you," he mumbled.

"Your starting date is next Monday, on the twenty-seventh. You are to go to the office on the first floor to receive your worker ID before you do anything else."

Josef nodded along dumbly. "Thank you. Bye."

When the phone clicked off, Dante was staring at Josef again. He just stared back at his father, not knowing what to say, what to think, how to even react, what facial expression to wear.

"Josef? Son, what is it?" Dante's gentle, rumbly voice seemed to have a magical effect on Josef. He immediately snapped out of it, jumping out of his seat with such force that he tipped over his chair and almost upended the table.

"I got the job!" he shrieked, his entire body shivering in excitement. Dante, much more calmly, stood up and walked over to his son. Josef was immediately enveloped by his father's giant, muscular arms. They were both smiling, Josef showing so much teeth that he felt almost ridiculous. And his father … Dante's shoulders were shaking.

"Dad?"

"I'm so happy for you, hatchling," he said with a voice choked by tears. He said that, and yet it was hard for Josef to believe him.

"Thank you." They stood there for a few more moments, and when they parted, Dante excused himself.

—·—

INTERLUDE 1: NOT MY NAME

His skin rippled beneath his fur.

"Darling, come here." The velvety, cold voice had his ears standing at attention. Darling felt another ripple tear through his body. It was painless, perfectly safe, and yet each time he did it he felt disgusted with himself. He felt the long, doe-brown fur along the entire length of his massive, soft body retreat into each individual follicle. His legs elongated; his joints cracked and snapped, rearranging themselves beneath his toughening skin. His face snapped back into a flatter shape, and the hair atop his head shot out to cover the two long, sensitive ears. Darling spat out a glob of mucus that tasted like hay, aiming right into the bin that sat beside Charles Young's desk.

He scratched with elongated claws at his exposed stomach. Young fed him too much in his rabbit form, but the weight looked lovely on his humanoid body. Darling also ran a hand through his long locks, untangling any stray hairs that often ended up as knots post-transition. Young didn't brush him, and his less-than-gentle stroking often left Darling's fur an absolute mess.

"Darling," Young hissed out. The man crawled on his hands and knees towards his master. His claws scraped at the linoleum floor of Young's office, and he felt his tail tickle the skin over his bare buttocks.

"Good boy." The perfectly manicured hand that descended from Young's desk scratched under his chin, and Darling wanted so badly to spit at him. The slight wetness underneath his thick beard made the fine hairs on the underside of his neck tangle, and Young seemed absolutely oblivious to the fact that it pulled at Darling's delicate skin. He hated having his scent glands scratched. He wasn't a dog.

"Wear this." Young dropped a shirt onto the floor before Darling. The shapeshifter grasped at it. His fingers were long and slender, but his thumbs were shorter and pulled too far back for him to comfortably grasp the shirt. It was white, standing out starkly against his long, auburn hair, and dark brown, lightly furred body. He left it unbuttoned; his fingers couldn't wrap around the hem of the shirt well enough to even attempt to button it. It didn't cover anything up, anyway; Young was a good head shorter than him and considerably leaner. His tail still brushed against his bare skin; his long, flat-footed legs stood out like wings on a fish. The shirt wrapped around him far enough to cover his breasts, but not enough to cover his large, soft stomach.

"Darling, stand up," Young cooed, brushing over Darling's velvety ears. He hated that name, but he had no other. Not like Shark.

He was a bit shaky when he stood up onto his legs. His large, furry feet stood firmly on the slippery floor, but his knees wobbled from the unfamiliar position, and his hips protested from the sudden straightening. Young didn't steady him, didn't help, just kept on staring into his computer.

Charles Young was a handsome man of a little over thirty years. He had a profile that could only be described as 'royal', with an aquiline nose, a rounded, dimpled chin, and a broad forehead. Face-on, he was even more handsome, with lips that looked sculpted out of rubies and amethyst pupils set into almond-shaped eyes. He had high cheekbones and a blemish-less face, with pearly white teeth and skin so fair that even Snow White would be jealous. And hair, hair so dark it reminded Darling of a black hole, brushed into a stylish swoop over his forehead. Darling didn't look at him for long.

"We're going to meet with my favourite subject today." Young smiled and it was blinding. There was nothing kind nor happy behind that smile. It didn't even reach his eyes.

***

Darling trotted after Young as they travelled through the Beneath, meandering in the halls of the HEL Facility. The Health Evaluation Laboratories, situated somewhere within the roots of the FCMC Behemoth, housed the newcomers. Each and every magical being that came in recently and was yet to have a treatment plan decided upon.

"Hold it down, don't let it bite you!" Young screamed at the young nurse that grasped at Darling's flailing limbs. Darling was spitting and hissing, and Young just stared at him with so much hatred in his eyes. The grip upon his left leg was inhuman; Darling could feel the bones shift and crack as he tried to buck, kick him off, do something.

"Darling, don't fall behind," Young hissed.

Darling hid his face beneath his long lengths of hair, ripping his eyes off the examination table covered in claw marks and deep grooves. Why it was still there, he would never understand.

The guards at the door nodded at Young. They had batons and tasers, dressed in thick garments and bulletproof vests. They each also wore protective talismans upon their persons, horseshoes and silver, and whatever else they thought that week would prevent them from being mutilated by a pissed off minor god.

"Sir." The guard on the left, a broad-shouldered man with a thick, white scar marring his dark cheek, nodded at Young. The other guard, a blond-haired woman with perpetually downturned, angry-looking eyebrows, leered over at Darling. Her smile showed too much teeth, too many fangs that made her look ravenous. The man to her left didn't skip a beat either, appraising Darling beneath the thin cotton shirt that he wore. He tried to pull the shirt tighter around himself, but he could still feel their eyes stick to his thick, naked thighs.

Once Young was through the double-barred doors and Darling was still outside with the guards, he let himself grunt at the two of them, thumping his feet in warning. The man just chuckled.

"Are you angry, little bunny?" the woman cooed, reaching out to stroke his head. She didn't even have time to get up onto her toes before Darling dipped through the doorway and attached himself to Young's side.

A wash of cold air greeted him, seeping underneath his skin. Young was grinning at him. His arm snaked around Darling's waist, while his hand rubbed the side of his neck. He hated the fact that the petting felt good, that Young's body against his was warm.

"Did those two guards scare my little Darling? Don't worry, I'll deal with them." The purr in Young's voice was almost tangible, and Darling felt as if his skin was being coated in a film of something slimy and sticky wherever Young touched him.

"Oi, hands off him, you creep." The new voice was loud and reverberated within the small room, penetrating Darling to the bones. Young immediately snapped to attention, pulling himself away from Darling with something that could almost be called disgust.

"Subject-20-465, you're awake." Young placed his arms behind his back, straightening his spine and pushing his chest out. The grey button-up did very little to hide his body, although there really wasn't much to look at. Young was a thin, gangly man with the physique of a teenager but the appetite of a geriatric dieter. He was neither very tall, nor very broad, nor very muscular. Physically, he wasn't imposing at all, no matter how he carried himself.

"Young," hissed Shark. The emaciated figure within the cage was pressed up against the bars. Their pale skin was going red from where the bars dug into their chest. Their ribs stood out horrifically, and their sunken-in face upon a long, bony neck always had Darling shivering beneath his fur. Their unblinking, endless eyes stared right at Young, stuck within a frame of sunken-in eye sockets.

"How are you feeling today, Subject-20-465?"

The being behind the bars was almost like a twisted, mirror reflection of Young. They both had skin so pale it was almost translucent, and long, black hair that seemed to suck in all of the light around it. They both had high cheekbones, a dimpled chin, and perfectly sculpted ruby lips. Young was smiling with his pearly white teeth, while the other had their lips pulled back in a snarl that showed a mouth full of shark-like fangs. And their eyes ...

"That is *not my name*!" the figure roared, and the lights above them blinked and flickered.

Young carried on smiling, his eyes perfectly still as he stared into the eyes of the figure. "Would you prefer Shark, then? Isn't that what some of my workers have started calling you?"

Shark's lips pulled back so far that Darling could see all of their grey, blood-less gums, a serpentine tongue flickering out to lick at their cracked, dry lips. Their eyes were open so wide that Darling thought he should be able to see the entire universe within them.

"That is NOT MY NAME!" The next roar shook the very foundation of the room, and bits of plaster rained down upon his and Young's heads. Darling covered his head with his arms, pressing his ears tightly against the sides of his face. He could still hear the roar reverberating in his head, bouncing off the walls of his ear canals.

"Well, you have to pick one or the other, my dear," Young continued, completely unaffected. "You know that you can't intimidate me into saying it. I own you, Shark. Your body, your soul, your power, and your name."

Shark grasped at the bars of their cage with their long, clawed hands. "How's Thlayli doing?" Their voice went soft, so quiet that Darling wondered if Young actually heard it.

Young's smile dropped, his small, manicured hands bunching up the fabric of his dress trousers. "His name is *Darling*."

This hiss was not a warning, as all the others were. This one was a promise.

Shark pulled their lips away from their teeth in something that almost resembled a smile. "That shirt suits you, Big Guy." Their black, endless eyes were trained on Darling, and he felt the cheeks of his human form grow warm. He, cowering behind the much smaller, much weaker, Charles Young, could no longer look at the one person within this facility he could trust. Because he knew that Shark could not trust him.

"Subject-20-465, I see that the wounds from your previous punishment have already healed. I think you won't mind another one."

Darling was shaking but not from the cold, digging his fingers into the thin fabric of the trousers. He couldn't look at Shark but knew that their eyes were still on him. Those eyes always stared, always looked, never blinking. They saw right into his soul.

"Sure. Bring it on, Charlie."

Darling was already at the door, ready to run out through it, back to the safety of Young's office, when he heard the almost imperceptible whisper meant for his ears only. "I'll see you later, Thlayli."

6

RED AND GOLD HORNS

On Monday, the twenty-seventh, Vanja dropped Josef off at the FCMC building for his first day at work. Vanja agreed to have Spot stay over; she worked from home, after all, and Josef even managed to persuade her to drive him around every so often. It was a deal that largely only benefited him, but she didn't seem to mind.

Inside the building, the receptionist from his interview was still there, her perfectly red nails still scratching at the corner of her perfectly red lips. When she noticed him, she almost jumped out of her seat.

"Josef! Welcome back!" She gave him a big smile and her brown eyes crinkled at the edges. Her blonde hair was braided into a pair of plaits that were wound around the base of her horns, and the rest of her horns were decorated by golden bangles. He realised that her plump cheeks were naturally rosy without the use of makeup; the lipstick and eyeshadow seemed to work perfectly with her olive skin.

"Nice jewellery," he huffed, feeling the air within his gullet growing warmer.

"Knew you'd like it, dragon-eyes." She giggled, giving him a wink. Josef coughed, huffing out a little burst of smoke.

"Dragon-eyes?" He pushed the glasses further up his nose.

"Oh, I'm just messing with you." She giggled again, and Josef had to wonder what changed between his last meeting with her and his current one. He didn't even know her name.

"You knew I would be in today?" he asked, trying to change the subject. Her cheeks went even more rosy.

"I've access to all the timetables." Her voice was soft and quiet. The blush only deepened. Josef decided to drop the subject, asking, instead, where he was supposed to pick his ID up from.

"First floor, office 4A," the receptionist trilled, and just as Josef was about to leave, she shouted after him, "My name is Phoebe, by the way!"

"Nice to meet you, I'm Josef!" A whine escaped his throat. *She knew that already!* He quickened his steps, tripping as he threw himself into the lift. This was going to be a long day.

***

Josef clipped the worker ID onto his lanyard, then spun it around so that no one could see his photo. They never let you wear glasses for your ID photos, and he never really understood it. What was the purpose behind it? To prevent light glares? He wore sunglasses; his glasses quite literally were there to prevent light glares. It annoyed him so much that ...

Josef felt his shoulder hit something, and a small man bounced back with a grunt.

"Oh, sorry."

Josef found himself face to face with a short, thin, handsome man. His dark hair was perfectly styled to fall gracefully across his forehead, his purple eyes shimmered like gemstones, and his lips, pulled down in a frown, were so red, naturally crimson, that they looked delicious. Josef felt himself blush and internally kicked himself for being so careless.

"Be careful where you walk. I don't tolerate daydreamers."

In that moment, Josef felt the fire within his belly extinguish itself. With cold, hard eyes, Charles Young looked up at him. His boss, *that* Charles Young.

"Sir! I'm so sorry! I didn't mean to! If I knew it was you, I would ... "

Mr Young thrust a hand up in front of his face. "Who are you?" Mr Young's perfectly manicured hand hovered before Josef's eyes as he gasped for air, trying to recall a single word within his scattered brain.

"Josef Braun. I ... I mean, nephew of Josef Braun. Josef Brooke Ryan, the new Junior Caretaker. Sir!" His back shot up; his shoulders pulled back. *What am I doing? I'm not in the damn army*, Josef admonished himself. In moments like these he was thankful that he was just enough dragon to not sweat.

"The new Junior Caretaker? Perfect!" Mr Young's handsome face immediately dropped the frown, and a beautiful smile replaced it. It didn't quite reach his shining eyes, but the curve of his red lips twisted above his perfect teeth had Josef feeling hot in ways that he didn't quite mind.

Mr Young turned on his heel, and Josef realised with horror that he couldn't take his eyes off his boss' shapely backside.

"Come along, nephew of Josef Braun. If you are working for me, you must have learned a thing or two from your uncle, right?"

Josef's long legs tangled beneath him as he tried to catch up to his boss. "Yes, sir! My Uncle Josef is the reason I decided to pursue magizoology."

Although Mr Young was a full head and some shorter than him, Josef felt minuscule. When Mr Young smiled at him, looking down at him from beneath his long, black lashes, his dragon flame grew so big within him that it began burning at the edges of his gullet.

"How quaint, being named after your famous uncle." A perfectly white canine bit into the succulent flesh of Mr Young's bottom lip. Josef wanted to kick himself.

"I'm actually named after both my uncles." When Mr Young turned away, Josef smacked himself on the forehead, twice or so before Mr Young looked back at him.

"So you're Josef Jr?"

Josef nodded quickly, feeling as if his brain was bouncing around in his skull from the force of it.

"Then I hope you are his junior in more than just name."

Josef didn't even notice when they began climbing down into the depths of the FCMC building, descending staircase after staircase, the blinding yellow lamps above them hanging on thin cables. They swung like trees in a storm, and the further down they went, the more Josef registered the gentle shivering of the earth, the quakes that tested the foundations of the rooms they were passing through. With each storey they descended, Josef also noticed a buzzing in the air, a continuous noise whose source he could not place. It grew louder and louder, until it was so loud that Mr Young handed him a set of bright orange ear plugs. Putting them in, Josef noticed the clear pieces of plastic sitting, almost invisible, within Mr Young's ear canals.

"Now, Josef Braun's nephew," Mr Young began at a semi-yell— the buzzing was getting so loud already— "what I need you to do is employ some of your uncle's disciplinary tactics! I am sure you have worked with naughty and rambunctious hellhounds before. This will be no different, I assure you!"

Josef's brain was running a mile a minute, turning towards his stores of knowledge. It was an automatic response, and yet a part of his brain was rebelling, asking 'why?' A part of him wanted to know what this was about, why Mr Young was in

45

need of disciplinary measures of all things. Who or what was he to discipline?

"Ready, Mr Ryan?" A door stood before him, Mr Young's hand placed on the handle. It was thick and double-barred, made of something that smelled like gold but was harder than steel. Above the door, Josef spied the words 'Health Evaluation Laboratories, Level 5 Containment Chamber' written in a bright, but fading, white. Standing there, the orange earplugs uncomfortably squished into his ears, the buzzing had become a roar. A literal roar, Josef realised, the continuous angry howl of a beast. Whether it was a roar of fear, anger, or pain, he couldn't quite tell.

"I'm ready, Mr Young." The door opened, and Josef felt a piercing cold escape through the door. The walls were covered in a thick layer of frost, and the five guards standing in a star shape in the centre of the room were dressed as if they were about to embark on a journey to the farthest reaches of Antarctica.

Josef stepped into the room and brushed a snowflake off his shoulder. It melted into a puddle the moment it made contact with his skin, only to freeze again before it even hit the floor. He noticed that the five guards in the centre were frozen to the floor, unfrozen only from the waist up.

They each held a larger version of a catchpole, the loops overlapping upon the body of an emaciated being. The being had black fur that seemed to eat up all the light around it. It was half upright, with digitigrade legs and a tail like a crocodile, its front paws extending from a barrel-like torso. Josef could count each of its ribs beneath its fur. Its face reminded him of a horse, but with a mouth full of three rows of shark-like teeth, and bloody-red horns burst out of its forehead. It was no creature he had ever seen before, and yet when it twisted to face him, he thought he recognised it. From its jaw dripped down saliva swathed by a freezing mist, like liquid nitrogen, and clouds of warm air were puffing out from its flaring nostrils. Its eyes were endless, black with swirls of purples and blues and speckles of white, as if he was looking into the sky above his uncles' cottage.

Those were the same eyes he saw on the kitten.

"Mr Ryan!" Mr Young placed a hand on his shoulder, his velvety voice rising above the crying of the beast. "Now is the time for you to use your skills!"

Josef nodded, not paying much attention to what Mr Young actually said. The hand on his shoulder pushed him forward, and Josef took a tentative step. The beast was panting, and yet also howling without pause. He saw long welts across its back when it twisted and turned, trying to rip itself out of the metal loops binding its body. There was a loop around each of its legs, one on each of its paws, and one wound tightly around its neck. Only its tail was free to swing wildly, following the motions of its body like a pendulum.

"Loosen the bonds!"

The guards all turned their heads to stare at him, each wearing an identical look of incredulity, noticeable even beneath their balaclavas.

"Do as he says." Mr Young's voice cut through the howling, and his warm breath ghosted over Josef's neck. The guards relented, each loosening the loops with shaking hands. Once free, the beast ripped the catchpoles off itself, tossing the instruments across the room to shatter into minuscule shards of ice.

Josef took the opportunity while it was distracted to pull a piece of coal out of his pocket. He tossed it between his hands for a few seconds, making sure that it was sufficiently extinguished, before he knelt and rolled it across the floor. The beast turned when the little, black ball stopped by its feet. The beast's endless, starry eyes focused on the coal, and Josef was shocked to learn that the coal's light didn't reflect off of them. It was as if those eyes held the actual stars within their confines.

Josef could feel the guards all holding their breaths, and Mr Young at his back was all taut like a spring. He was the only one who was relaxed, watching as the creature before them bent down, poking at the coal with one big claw. A harder push sent the coal tumbling back over to Josef, who caught it with the inside of his shoe. The creature waited, poised, and Josef didn't disappoint when he kicked the coal back over. Josef and the creature passed the coal between each other like a football, until the little ball had rubbed off almost completely on the floor. The ice separating them was covered in a large, black smudge, and the remains of the ball crumpled when Josef tried kicking it back again.

The creature was no longer looking at the remains of its toy. Its eyes were pointed right into Josef's own. He knew it wasn't possible, but, in that moment, it felt as if that penetrating, endless gaze could look straight through his glasses and right into his soul.

He didn't know how long he held that gaze, how long the creature before him tore him apart from the inside, judging every little bit that made him *him*. He came to at the moment that the connection was broken, those starry eyes disappearing from his field of view, taken over by an open, pinkish maw full of rows of sharp teeth. A second later, Josef heard the scream, and this time knew that it was one of pain. He saw an arc of lightning race through the air, dimming the glaring, white lamps above them.

"Wait! Stop it!" It was his voice that spoke, but he didn't recognise it. It was his body that moved towards the convulsing, foaming-at-the-mouth creature, but he didn't register the movements until he was already by its side. Its claws made deep grooves in the floor of the chamber, its giant tail flailing madly as it beat dents into the metallic surface.

Josef felt a hand on his shoulder, and a firm grip pulled him backwards. "Very well done, Mr Ryan," Charles Young's voice purred in his ear, and it had him shivering.

"Why are you doing this?" The tears choked him; he felt his throat clench around words he didn't know he was brave enough to say. There was something in Mr Young's expression that he couldn't place, a quality to his frown that Josef wasn't good at discerning.

"Believe me, Mr Ryan. I want this about as much as you do. But there are sacrifices I must make for the safety of my staff and of all the other subjects at the facility. This is an unfortunate unpleasantness that we just have to live with." He said it with such conviction, his voice so calm and steady. His amethyst eyes were twinkling prettily, and Josef forgot where he had left his voice.

"I believe you," he choked out eventually, when Charles Young wrapped his small hand around Josef's bicep and began leading him away with a smile.

"Of course you do, Mr Ryan. I'm your boss, after all."

7

STARLIGHT POLLUTION

Josef didn't go to see Vanja when he got home that day. When she didn't reply to his text that he was on his way, he figured she was already asleep, and Spot not far behind her. Instead, he climbed up to the roof of his apartment complex.

From the roof, he could see an endless black void yawning above him. The light pollution from the city streets was cruel, only allowing the grinning moon to pierce through the darkness above. Back in the cottage where his uncles lived, the stars were like spotlights shining down onto the earth below. Here, in the city, the spotlights came from far off streetlamps and office buildings. It often made him think— imagine that they were alone. The denizens of Earth, abandoned by the universe, unaware that they were the last beings in existence, that it wasn't just the glare of streetlights that made the stars disappear from the sky. In the dead of night, when most people were asleep, all the shops were closed, and only the occasional car ran past his hanging feet, Josef imagined that he was the last being in existence. Sometimes, he even started to believe it.

"You're back late." Vanja's voice was thick with sleepiness, but it still managed to startle Josef out of his daydream.

"I'm back on time," he huffed, taking her hand and helping her sit down. "You just fell asleep early." Her lipstick was smudged, and her eyes were blurry.

"Spot is very energetic, she had me running around all day." She hid a yawn behind a dainty, pale hand.

"Do you miss the stars?"

"Silly question, Brooke. I don't miss stars. I miss their reflection in water, in lakes and rivers and seas."

"Right, rusałka blood."

"Yes. Water creature, not sky creature like you dragon types."

"You still miss it, don't you?"

"Yes. Boo, are you taking my attention off today? I want to ask how today went."

"It went ... fine."

"Tell me, Brooke."

"Why do you always call me Brooke, Rus?"

"Because you are as much Brooke as you are Josef. I am making up for all people who only see you as Josef, nephew of Josef Braun. You are also Brooke! Son of Elspeth Ryan and Dante Rubino! Nephew of Brooke Ryan! Brother of Jozić Vanja!"

"You don't have to shout, Vanja, I can hear you." He laughed, throwing a hand over her shoulders. Her head thunked against the side of his neck and it hurt, but they were both laughing so it was okay .

"You are Josef Brooke Ryan, not just one or other. And Josef Brooke Ryan just got his first proper job, so tell Oh Great Vanja all about it."

"My weightlifting *was* a proper job." He pouted. "But, anyway. I fell in love with my boss after falling *into* him, and then had to 'discipline' a creature I have never seen before, because it was acting out."

"I … what?"

"I had to 'discipline' … "

"No! You fell for your boss? Brooke! You are worse than me!"

"I didn't know he was my boss, at first! And— and I don't even control who I fall in love with!"

"Oh, Brooke, Brooke. Diamond earring guy not good enough for you?"

"I didn't end up getting his number … And it's not like I'm going to start dating my boss! Just … quietly crushing on him."

"Booooooo. I need to get you boyfriend. Maybe take you to some event, have you meet people."

"Vanja."

"What?"

"Shut up."

"Ah, you're grumpy because you're lonely. Don't worry, Oh Great Vanja will help you."

"I'm leaving."

"Wait! Don't leave me on edge!"

"On the edge, Vanja!"

"That what I said!"

"Ugh."

— · —

Interlude 2: The Man in the Glasses

Young didn't leave him alone often. Sometimes, Young would need to be present Above. Above the roots of the FCMC, he had an office, he had workers, he had to be present. Darling wasn't allowed Above. Only the most senior of staff could come down to the trailing hallways Beneath that Darling was allowed to occupy, and all the other workers never crossed his path.

The man with the glasses was the first one in years whom Darling did not recognise. He didn't know the names of all the workers, but he could recognise them. Their voices, their smells, to some degree the way they looked as well.

The man with the glasses smelled like the firebreathers Young kept in the deepest parts of the underground. He had a gentle voice, and he was handsome in a way that Darling didn't see often. He was new, completely and utterly new. And yet Darling saw him trotting behind Young like a lovesick puppy, descending into the bowels of the Behemoth. They were heading towards Shark.

Whenever Young was gone, Darling refused to stay in his rabbit form. He was a simple woodland shifter, a forest nymph in possession of only two forms, both of which he felt comfortable wearing. However, the lack of thumbs proved annoying, even if his great bulk made it easy to rifle through Young's desk. He never knew what he was looking for; he never really looked for anything specific. Reading didn't come easily to him, so files and memos were useless to him. With a lack of reading skills, he didn't need to look for writing utensils either. He was fed enough, and Young didn't leave any clothes in his office.

Darling liked pictures. Young often had pictures in his desk, hidden in the folds of white sheets of paper. There were photos that had Shark on them, photos of other subjects, front-facing photos of different workers.

Young was predictable, and Darling knew how to read him well. There, beneath pages upon pages of scrawls that Darling couldn't read, he saw the photo of the man with the glasses. Except he had no glasses, and his intelligent, reddish eyes glared up at Darling from the photograph.

Darling grasped a piece of paper, a slip that Young wouldn't miss. He pressed it against the first word he saw, standing out in bold, black letters above the photo of the man with the reddish eyes. He used his nail, instead of a pen, to scratch the word into the paper, tracing it over the black letters he could just barely see beneath the white sheet.

Then he returned to his rabbit form. His thick, furry dewlap functioned as a pocket, the small slip of paper pressed between his chin and the sack of fat.

***

The Beneath was completely underground. There were no windows, and the lights from the walls were a glaring yellow and hanging off chains. But there was circulation of fresh air throughout the entire labyrinth of rooms and hallways. The vents that allowed for said circulation were too small for a human to crawl through, big enough for something smaller to crawl through, but screwed tightly to the walls. Darling had the opposable thumbs to unscrew the vents and the smaller, fluid body that let him crawl through them, dragging his belly over the metal floors. All the vents were connected in a network that spanned the entire length and width that the Beneath covered, letting him reach anywhere within the building that he wished.

The room that Shark lived in outside of 'testing' was somewhere within the centre of the entire network but situated on the lowest floor of the entire complex. The air within the room was cold but crackling with energy. Through the thin grate of the vent, Darling could see Shark. They were leaning against a wall in the large room, barred off from a massive, crackling generator. A single, thin cable reached over from the sparking arcs of lightning and the blue, cold light of the bulbs, snaking its way across the floor. It slipped through the bars in the centre of the room, trailing a path up Shark's leg, up their naked body, to the collar digging into their pale throat.

Darling began scratching at the grating, long claws letting out clanking sounds against the thin metal. Shark's eyes shot open, and the galaxies within them settled upon the vent. Gently, slowly, Darling pressed his chin against the grate, pushing with his shoulders until he could feel the slip of paper rest between the plates of the grating. He finished pushing it through with a gentle nudge of his nose.

He saw the paper fall in dancing arcs, gently cascading down onto the floor. It suddenly went careening towards Shark, fluttering with such fervour that Darling feared it would rip. But it slowed, and it rested softly between Shark's legs. They snapped the paper up, licking their lips with a forked tongue.

"His name is Brooke, then." The smile upon their lips was almost sweet, their eyes softening at the mention of the man with the glasses: Brooke, as Darling now knew to call him.

"You did well, Thlayli, my friend." Their eyes met through the grate. "I think, with him, we might have a chance." If only Darling believed it. Shark had said the same thing so many times before, so many plans they had created. And yet they were still here.

"Go back now. Before Young catches you."

***

The return journey was faster than the first trip, Darling no longer having to worry about losing the slip of paper squirrelled away into the folds of his dewlap. He got back to the office just in time to screw the vent grate back in place, tossing the screwdriver into the mounds of pillows and blankets that functioned as his resting area. Then, with a quick step and his head held high, Young marched into the office.

He didn't say a thing to Darling, didn't even look in his direction, as he fell into his desk chair with a sigh. His entire body went boneless, and he puffed out a breath of air to relocate a lock of hair that had hung before his eyes. These were the moments Darling hated the most, the moments where Young acted the most human, reminding Darling that this wasn't a robot that he was trapped with, programmed to cause pain and fear. This was a human, with a premeditated want to hurt him. He had feelings, emotions, he knew exactly what he was doing to Darling.

"I can't stand them," Young huffed, and Darling felt the need to hide himself. "What a damn annoyance. They work for me, *me*! Not anyone else. They're supposed to listen to me! I *own* them, for fuck's sake! And now they're defying my orders and overloading the generators again! If I didn't need them so much,

Welei would already be dead! Stupid creature, getting in my fucking way! How am I supposed to get those drake skulls to that jeweller *now*? How am I supposed to transport the damn unicorns to the butcher? Don't they know how much energy it takes to trap those damned cockatrices for those stupid cock fights? They're ruining *everything*!" Young burst out of his seat, his voice rising until it was painful to listen to. Darling wanted to hide even more, digging his claws into the linoleum floor, his ears standing at attention. That name, it felt wrong, like something he wasn't supposed to hear, something he shouldn't know.

That name was what he needed. He didn't know how he was supposed to get it, but he needed it.

Young dug into his desk, pulling out a small, black rectangle, pressing a button on the side of it.

"Reminder." His voice was unpleasantly husky as he spoke into the small recorder. "Up the dosage of Subject-20-465's tranquillizers while in the generator cell. Until the new trainer works out how to subdue them, it's best they're kept on a higher dose, fuck the fact it messes with their energy levels."

The recorder returned to the desk, and Darling felt his heart sink.

They would never get out.

8

THE BEGINNING OF THE UNIVERSE

The next day, Josef woke up with a spicy taste on his tongue. Vanja had treated him to a late dinner of curry. She didn't make it, thank the ancestors, and they were able to have a nice chat over reheated curry leftovers before Josef had to nod off after a long day at work. Since it was a Tuesday, and Josef didn't have to work, they had breakfast together, taking Spot out for a long walk near Déjà Brew. Their conversation eventually fell upon the creature Josef had to deal with the day before.

The creature still eluded him. No mythical being he knew lined up one-to-one with the curious amalgamation he had met the day before. Vanja had no ideas, other than one.

"Maybe it is old god? Lots of old gods were shapeshifters who took on animal characteristics. Egyptian gods had heads of animals. Norse gods and Greek gods could shapeshift into animals."

Josef replied with a sigh, "But we haven't found any proof for the existence of old pagan gods. If any existed, they were most likely wiped out long ago. And what gods do you know of that can create ice, but also have eyes like a galaxy and the head of a horse?" She didn't have a response to that, and they moved on to different topics.

***

On Wednesday, Josef arrived at the FCMC building and immediately went to say hi to Phoebe. She wore gold again and smiled at him so widely that it made him feel odd.

"Busy day today!" She giggled as he swiped himself in. "Mr Young wants you down below again. It seems that you have made an impression on him, dragon-eyes."

Josef pushed his glasses further up his nose, looking away from her. "He wants me downstairs? Really?"

Phoebe nodded, her grin even wider, her eyes trying to catch his through the slivers between the frames and his face. He nodded at her politely, gave her a kind smile, and marched towards the elevator.

He met Mr Young at the second to lowest level. Mr Young looked as radiant and handsome as ever, and yet the smile he gave Josef still didn't reach his eyes.

"Mr Ryan. This way. After your performance on Monday, I'm sure you will be glad to know that you are on your way to being promoted to Senior Caretaker. I'm sure this is a shock to you, this only being your second day, but I've been looking for someone like you for years. Years! Someone who knows how to deal with all manner of beings, who can so easily calm down a raging beast. Our little issue has stumped hundreds of other trainers, but *you* are a *natural*. I don't care how you did it, but if you can work your magic again, I'm sure there is more than just a promotion waiting in your future." Mr Young didn't let him get a word in, although Josef had nothing to say in the first place. A promotion. Already. Based on a single day of work and a single show of skill. A promotion.

"Thank you, Mr Young," he mumbled, trying not to stumble either over his words or over his feet.

"Don't thank me. Thank them." The same double-barred door from Monday opened before him. The 'them' Mr Young referred to, as they both stepped into the cold room, was an emaciated, skeletal figure with pale, translucent skin, sitting behind a set of bars bisecting the room. They had their back turned to him and Mr Young, but Josef could still see their long, black hair trailing down from their shoulders; the digitigrade legs were covered in a layer of black fur that they sat upon. They didn't turn, and Mr Young didn't say anything to them.

He turned once more to Josef. "Think of them as a particularly intelligent dog, like a hellhound. I want them eating out of the palm of your hand and walking at your heel as soon as possible. Have I made myself clear?"

Josef nodded, watching Young do a half pirouette and begin to walk out.

"Oh, and Mr Ryan. *Don't* listen to what they say. They're very gifted in mimicry."

And then Josef was alone with the being.

"Hello, Brooke." Their voice was melodic and velvety. They turned their face towards him, and a pair of black, bottomless eyes stared back at him. Their mouth was full of shark-like teeth, just like before. Their face was intersected by two long, bleeding slashes, carved into their thin skin in an X shape, and their neck was wrapped in a thick, leather collar.

"You know my name." Josef swallowed, taking a step back from the creature. He had heard of beings capable of reading his mind and of those capable of mimicking human speech. Something wasn't adding up, however. Josef knew, from dealing with harpies before, the more beastly cousins of sirens, that a being capable of mimicry did not possess humanoid vocal cords. Their voices never sounded quite right.

"Yes. I do. My name is ... I go by Shark. There, now we're even." Their smile was handsome, even if their raised lips twisted the scars upon their face. That velvety, melodic voice spoke with a resonance unique to humanoid vocal cords, something his ancestors had meticulously evolved within themselves. Something that no mere mimic could replicate. Something no mere hellhound trainer had any right to know. Josef knew the shame of having knowledge above his station, and yet ...

"Does that hurt?" He approached Shark, taking steady steps towards them. Young was a businessman; Josef was sure he was simply provided with incorrect information about how to care for this creature. He could fix that, he *would* fix that.

Shark fluttered their eyelashes, leaning more heavily against their bars. "It's excruciating." Josef thought that he saw a star falling within the depths of Shark's galaxy eyes. He noticed that they were shivering, but he wasn't sure if it was from the pain or the cold. He knelt either way, shrugging his blazer off his shoulders and placing it around Shark's prone form. He had to stretch his arms through the bars that separated them, reaching over with the sleeve of his dress shirt to wipe, ever so gently, at the whispers of blood that dripped from their face.

"I don't know why I'm here," Josef began when he realised that Shark wasn't going to speak, "but I want to help you." He could feel the fire within his belly growing warmer.

"I love your eyes." Shark's voice was so quiet, Josef wasn't sure if he heard them right. Something, however, compelled him to reach up, putting his dark lenses away into his pocket. His eyes met the endless reach of Shark's galaxies, and he felt as if he was falling.

"I love yours too."

Shark's nose scrunched up as they smiled, and the corners of their eyes crinkled. Their lips were a dark, juicy red, and they reminded him of Mr Young's lips. That was when he realised that Shark looked nearly identical to Mr Young.

"This face is my own, believe me, Brooke." The sincerity of their voice, the only sound that Josef heard anymore, took his breath away.

"I believe you."

Shark seemed to catch their breath, their chest stuttering with their words. "Thank you. I'm glad someone does."

Josef swallowed thickly, his head growing fuzzy, and all that he could say was, "Yeah." His limbs felt leaden, refusing to obey him as he was compelled to move forward, enraptured by the swirling stars within Shark's eyes.

"Kiss me." He pressed himself against the bars, and they reached out through the bars to grasp his hands to steady him, and their hands were *freezing*. Josef leaned over until his face rested against the bars. The cold metal between them was a buffer, but the warmth of their shared mouths was sweet and comforting. Their lips were as soft as he thought they would be. Josef could feel the tension escaping from Shark's shoulders, travelling up their throat and escaping through their open mouth. In a distant part of his brain, he worried about the wrongness of this, the fear of Young finding them overpowering the haze within his mind. But even as his eyes cleared, he leaned further into the kiss, finding comfort in another warm body, in being *wanted* for what felt like the first time in years.

Their kiss was short but meaningful, and Josef believed, for a moment, that this was the end of the world, that this was everything there was in the universe, and that when they separated, everything would end. But when they did, he realised that the universe had just begun.

He held onto that feeling for the rest of the day.

9

TREASURED TIME

Josef worked twelve-hour days, from 6:00 a.m. to 6:00 p.m., Monday, Wednesday, and Friday. That sort of schedule suited him very well. It gave him time to take care of Spot, hang out with Vanja, read.

It gave him a lot of time to read.

***

When he came in to work on Friday, Phoebe wasn't there. He didn't even notice it, with his nose stuck to the pages of a book, until he was almost at the elevator and the receptionist hadn't beamed at him and told him 'Hi'.

Unobstructed by small talk, although slightly dejected at Phoebe's absence, he descended in the elevator with his face pressed into his book.

"What'chu reading, Cookie?" Shark hummed as Josef made his way towards the barred-off half of the room.

"I told you not to call me that, Shark," he grumbled, still not pulling his face out of the book. "Just because it rhymes with 'Brookie' doesn't make it not sound ridiculous." The shapeshifter giggled, and the sound was melodic. It almost sounded inhuman, inorganic. Like a windchime dancing with the wind as a bird sung from the branches above it. The shiver it elicited from Josef made Shark grin, and when he finally put the book down, he saw that grin only widen.

"You're reading up on old gods. Have you become religious, Brooke?"

Josef knelt before them, sliding the book to the back of the room. Their hands immediately encircled his neck, pulling him down further and squishing his face against the bars. His glasses discarded, they kissed, and it was even better than the first day.

"I'm just doing some research, *mi tesoro*." The pet name seemed to go down well, if the fireworks in Shark's eyes were anything to go by.

"Tell me all about it."

And he did. For countless hours, Josef talked. He talked so much that his throat hurt by the end of the day. He told Shark everything, from his research to his favourite pastimes, to his Uncle Josef who instilled a love for magizoology within him. And all the while, Shark listened, tracing their hands up and down his body, exploring him and loving him.

Josef talked, and his hands were busy with a small first aid kit he had snuck in. He swiped the antiseptic cloth over Shark's face with gentle strokes, bestowing kisses upon their face every time they flinched. And still he talked, and he explored their naked body. Each bruise, he kissed; each bleeding wound, he patched up. Each time he came upon a new wound, Shark's body froze within his grasp, their chest hitching and their eyes slamming shut. Each time he swiped the antiseptic wipe over these new wounds, rubbed cream into a yellowing bruise, or placed a plaster over a cut, Shark melted into his grip, their muscles becoming pliant beneath their taut skin.

Eventually, they were both sitting sideways against the bars, their shoulders pressed closely together. Shark wore Josef's coat, snuggling into it despite not needing the warmth. Josef had taken off his shirt on Shark's earlier behest and was sitting with his chest on full display, the scars and the freckle-like scales that dotted his skin being peppered by kisses.

"You wanted to ask me something when you first came in." They already knew how to read him, and he had no clue how. Their voice was thick with sleepiness, but it was still a good few hours before Josef had to go home. He hadn't even noticed the time, not when Shark began telling him about their life prior to the FCMC. A cottage in the Scottish countryside, fresh milk every day and their own little vegetable garden.

"I ... meant to ask you what you are." It seemed silly, now that he had said it out loud.

"Well, what are you, Brooke?"

"I'm two-quarters Irish, human. One-quarter Italian, also human. And one-quarter German, but this time dragon."

Shark hummed, and their fingers traced over the scaly skin on Josef's palms.

"Your beautiful eyes, they're from your dragon half, aren't they?" The glasses made by Uncle Brooke were somewhere on the floor between Josef and the door, and his russet eyes were staring right at Shark.

"The only part of me that gives it away, really." The laugh that came out of him was needlessly bitter, but he didn't seem to know how to stop it. "I'm ... too human for dragonkind, but too dragon for humankind. I don't fit in anywhere."

Shark's dark hair brushed against Josef's bare shoulder, and the weight of their head was almost comforting. "You're enough for me, fit in perfectly," they mumbled sleepily, pressing another kiss against a reddish scale beneath his collar bone.

"Fit in? Where?"

"With me." They pulled their head back up and their smile took Josef's breath away. "I don't fit in with humanity, or with all the humanoids like your rusałka friend Vanja. I ... I come from a planet in a different solar system, and the closest things I resemble on Earth are the fae. But I'm not fae, I'm an alien, born from a comet that came to Earth. Although, I'm not really an alien anymore. I've spent my entire life on Earth. I've spent the past forty-three years on Earth, since the day of my birth. Where do I fit in? Nowhere. Nowhere but with you." They reached their arm up and placed their palm against the bars. Josef did the same, and their skin was wonderfully cold compared to his perpetual warmth. His hands were bigger, broader, with longer claws he had always struggled to trim. Their hands were delicate and slender, but their thumb was considerably shorter than it would have been on a human, and their pointer finger was longer than their middle one. It was humanoid enough that you couldn't tell at first glance, and yet completely alien to him.

"You're perfect," he whispered.

"So are you." And this time, they did more than just kiss.

***

At 4:00 p.m., two hours before Josef was off work, his company-issued walkie-talkie buzzed.

"Shit, Shark, my coat!" Josef jumped up onto shaky legs, scanning the floor on his side of the room for his trousers. Shark was crawling and rolling across the floor, trying to get to the long-since-discarded coat.

"My body feels like jelly," they whined, their knees making 'thunk, thunk' sounds against the floor as they quickened their pace. The walkie-talkie flew across the room when Shark finally retrieved it, buzzing all the while. It perfectly missed the bars and landed in Josef's grasp as if deposited there purposefully.

Phoebe's voice briefly rang out from the walkie-talkie before the connection switched over to his cellphone, stuck up on the ground floor of the building. He hadn't expected anyone to call him at this hour, but he was glad the FCMC had ways to get around the lack of service down Beneath.

"Hello? Who is it?" Josef briefly cursed himself for not asking Phoebe what the number was.

"Hatchling? It's your father, how are you?" Dante's voice on the other line made Josef cringe. Not only because of what his father had interrupted, but also because of the weak, breathy way he sounded.

"I'm sorry, Dad, I was busy and don't have good service at my workplace." Out of the corner of his eye, Shark was shoving the coat back through the bars, their hands shaking slightly.

"Oh, should I call later?"

"No! It's okay, I just finished as you called." His hand flew to the microphone on his walkie-talkie when Shark burst out laughing, hoping that his father didn't hear it.

"Oh, is that Vanja there with you?" Dante sounded so hopeful, and Josef's heart broke. His father loved Vanja; she was the daughter he had always wanted. When his two children called together, it almost seemed to breathe new life into Dante.

"No, it's my ... my partner."

"Oh, hatchling, I'm so happy for you!"

From the middle of the room, Shark was beaming, their little, pale face pressed against the bars. Dante sounded as happy as Shark looked, and Josef's heart ached.

"Hey, Dad, would you like me to visit you?" Josef met Shark's eyes, and wished he had his glasses in that moment.

"Oh, no, it's alright. Spend time with your partner, hatchling, you're still young."

"Dad, you don't sound alright. Are you sure you don't want me to come stay with you at the cottage?"

Shark's face fell. Josef's heart beat an uncomfortable rhythm when he realised he couldn't tell what Shark's expression meant.

"I'm alright, hatchling. You don't have to come visit me at all."

"If you say so, Dad. I'll call you later, though, okay? And I'll remind Vanja to do the same." He smiled even though his father couldn't see him. Dante said a weak goodbye, and the walkie-talkie clicked, but Josef didn't pull it away from his ear for a long while.

"My love ... " Shark's arms were around him when he sat back down, their face pressed into his neck.

"I don't know what to do, Shark. I just don't know what to *do*."

INTERLUDE 3: THE MISTAKES OF THE PITIFUL

It was Sunday, and Darling was alone again. It was rare that Young would leave Darling by himself twice in one week. Brooke had to have made an impression on the cold, inhuman man, but Darling didn't care to find out what linked them.

Instead, he took the reprieve that Young's absence gave him. He went to visit Shark.

"Thlayli, I think I'm in love," Shark sighed, leaning against the nearby wall in a faux faint. "I've missed the touch, the presence of another sentient being. I missed the connection, this feeling. He fell into it so easily too, but now he holds me of his own volition! What a man ... "

Darling scratched at the grate of the vent, showing Shark that he was still listening. Shark's eyes seemed brighter, almost, as he watched them move around their cell. The reddish, angry wounds upon their face were almost fully healed already. There would be no scars.

"Saying it like that, maybe I'm just desperate for the contact. But, Thlayli, he understands me! He is struggling, and he has tough decisions to make, but he is so kind, so sweet." Shark was pacing their cell again. Darling wanted to scream, make some sort of noise, something between frustration and annoyance. Shark was walking, they were being active again, and yet the both of them were no closer to getting free, not even with the human man's help.

"He has something within him, I can feel it. He's the one, Thlayli, he is!" In that moment, Shark collapsed against the floor, and the door to the generator room burst open. Young marched in, holding a taser in one hand and a whip in the other. His eyes swivelled around the room, up the walls and across the ceiling. Darling curled up behind the grate, suddenly feeling his body freeze, as if paralysed. Why couldn't he move? Why couldn't he run away?

"What did you do, you fucking bitch?" Young yelled, and it was the first time in a long while that Darling had heard him raise his voice. He felt his heart thumping against his ribcage so fast, he was scared it would jump out of his chest.

"'Bitch' still isn't my name," Shark hissed from the floor, their body in a boneless sprawl. Their hair tastefully rested against their skin, hiding their most intimate parts beneath curtains of black tresses.

Young's face was red, and his lips were pulled back in a snarl, appearing thinner than normal. His cheeks weren't as defined beneath his reddish skin, his nose now shorter and flatter, his chin dimple-less. He raised his hand and the skin over his fingers was coarse and calloused, his fingernails jagged and torn.

The whip fell, the crack piercing Darling through the heart. It landed upon Shark's bare stomach, leaving a red valley that parted their white flesh. Their shriek was ear-piercing; the small whimpers coming from their clenched lips were animalistic. Another blow fell, and their hands tore at the metal floor of their cell, their legs going taut as they tried to push against the pain. Another blow made them choke on a sob, and the fourth one had them smashing their head against the floor. Another sob fell, followed by another whimper, and the four cuts on their abdomen wept. The blood stained their pale body, like painted, white roses, and they lay prone upon the floor for all to see them.

"Darling, to my office, now!"

The roar kick-started Darling's heart, sending him into a frenzy of flailing paws. The sound that he made as he galloped back through the metal vents was deafening.

***

Young already waited for him in the office. A kick to his soft belly had him rolling across the floor, flailing around as he tried to get his feet back under him. Young said nothing, but his face was back to its handsome state. His perfectly manicured hands grabbed Darling by one of his ears when he was done shifting. The pull against his scalp was excruciating. It was as if the very skin upon his head was being ripped open.

There was no shirt waiting for him when Young dragged him to his bed, forcing him to crawl on all fours across the floor. Another kick to his side had him curling up into a tight ball, pressing his hands against the tender spot. Young still didn't say a word. He never did, all punishments doled out by his own hand perpetually silent.

The next kick forced the air out of his lungs, and Darling could already feel the bruises forming. His throat burned and his eyes stung from the pain.

Young never hurt him too bad; he could take it. A few kicks and then he would be apologetic, that's always how it worked between the two of them, like an abusive relationship, like they were lovers that just couldn't stay away from each other at the end of the day. Darling took it obediently.

Young's eyes burned like dual, purple flames. Darling remembered hearing once that blue-purple flames were much, *much* hotter than a regular fire. And these purple flames were scorching, burning away at his resolve.

Another kick forced out of him a choking gasp. A thin stream of air sounding akin to a train whistle, forced out between his large front teeth. He couldn't breathe, his chest felt like it was about to cave in, his shuddering ribs rattling beneath his skin.

His throat kept burning, like he was choking on shards of his own ribcage alongside the strangled air his lungs couldn't quite expel.

He looked up at Young through the curtain of his hair hanging before his darkening eyes. The long tresses tickled his flat nose and the edges of his jaw, and it was something other than the pain that he could focus on. The corners of his vision were already black, and he was looking at that man through a pinprick of light. If he focused on the tickle of his hair against his skin, he could hang onto consciousness for a while yet, however precarious his connection was. Young stared down at him, his body slack, his eyes completely blank, almost glazed over. Darling didn't break eye contact, even if he couldn't be sure that Young actually saw him.

This little rebellion was his secret, his only reprieve; he was determined to hang onto it.

"Oh, Darling." Young's voice was barely above a whisper. He bent over, and Darling was sure that he could hear the way his breath rattled in his chest. A soft, manicured hand reached out and stroked over his ears. The little sigh which accompanied that action was almost euphoric, and Darling felt the urge to yank his head back.

"Poor thing, I won't hurt you."

You already did, he wanted to scream. Scream, cry, yell, even whisper. He wanted to tell Young exactly what he did, in a language he would understand.

Young scooted over, suddenly kneeling right before Darling's face. His gangly, thin arms wrapped as best as they could around Darling's Flemish bulk, and Darling let himself be guided. The man wanted Darling's head pressed against his collarbones, low enough that the tip of his ear brushed against where Young's heart should have been. The top of his head was pressed firmly, near painfully, against Young's chin. He could feel that pinprick of pain shoot through his spine, making his tail wag and tingle, and he wanted so badly to thump, to warn even *himself* of the danger he was now in.

Young's hands brushed over Darling's head, over his silken ears and down to the base of his neck. "I know you didn't mean to, my poor, little bunny," Young cooed. "That horrible, horrible creature brainwashed you, forced you to visit them. Completely against your will." Darling wanted to scream. "But you must understand, I'm only trying to protect you. Things of that kind can hurt you so easily, but I can tame them, I can force them to behave. I *will* force them to behave, eventually." Young's hands trailed down over his shoulders, smoothing down the ruffled fur on his back, going lower and lower. Darling stayed still, silent, when Young began fondling his tail, stroking up the entire length of it, as if it was something else he wanted to stroke. Darling felt sick.

"Shhh, I'll keep you safe." The breath on the back of his neck was warm, leaving tingling pinpricks wherever it ghosted over him. "I'll keep you safe from that monster. I'll make sure

Welei never touches you again. You're mine, Darling. Mine!" His hands left Darling's body in the blink of an eye, and cold air attacked him. Young was moving away from him, leaving him on the bed to shiver and shake. He was just an animal, after all. You don't touch your animals in that way. Not even Young would stoop that low.

Young left him alone in the office, still gasping for air. There was a click, and the buzzing static assaulting Darling's sensitive ears disappeared. He curled up around the little, black rectangle, its cold, plastic body warming up swiftly as it lay there, pressed against the side of his chest. He could feel his bones grating against each other as he breathed, and he realised with horror that something was broken.

He couldn't shift anymore.

10

GHOSTS OF OUR ANCESTORS

Josef came into work the next morning to Phoebe beaming. She was dressed, as always, in all red, but the golden accents she had taken to wearing had increased. She even had a golden nose ring in, and Josef wasn't sure if he remembered her wearing one previously.

"Not much for you to do today, dragon-eyes!" She beamed right up at him as he swiped his ID card. He let the ID swing free on its lanyard and looked at her with a quirked eyebrow.

"Not much work? I thought I was meant to be downstairs today again."

Phoebe's smile faltered a bit, but it was back on her face in seconds. "Well, Mr Young has different plans for you today. I heard that he personally changed your timetable." She fluttered her eyelashes, painted black, the only part of her makeup that wasn't red.

"Personally?"

"Yup." She popped the P as if she was popping a bubble gum bubble. "Which means you've got a free afternoon, dragon-eyes." Her facial expression changed. Her beaming smile turned softer, she angled her head downwards to look at Josef from beneath her eyelashes, her red lip caught between her small, pretty teeth. Josef noticed with a professional interest her lack of canines and how the rest of her teeth were even and uniform.

"I suppose I do," he mumbled, playing idly with his ID. Maybe he should call Vanja, have another meet up at Déjà Brew.

"So ... " Phoebe began, twirling a lock of blond hair around a red-painted finger, "I happen to have the afternoon free too."

Josef blinked, realising that she was still talking to him, so he smiled at her. "That's nice."

"Would you like to go out with me?" She blurted it out with such force that Josef took a step back. She leant over her desk, coming almost completely face to face with him, her cheeks burning almost as red as her lipstick.

"Phoebe ... I'm not attracted to women." He took another step back from her, not looking in her direction. She sank back into her seat in the corner of his eye, and her face seemed accepting, although maybe it was just sad.

"I'm sorry, I thought you liked me back." She sounded dejected, and Josef's head shot back up to look at her. He slipped his glasses off his nose, reaching around the computer at her desk to hold her hand.

"But I *do* like you, just as a friend. I'm sorry if I gave you the wrong impression, Phoebe. I'm autistic." She had pretty eyes. He could see them much better now without the blockade formed by his dark sunglasses. Those eyes were slightly wet, but they crinkled at the corners and Josef realised that she was smiling.

"Oh, it's not your fault, dragon-eyes. I'm like that too, and I don't always know how to take the hint." She was laughing now, wiping at her eyes as she let out small, wet chuckles. Josef squeezed her hand tighter.

"Learned how to flirt off the TV, huh?"

"Yeah, I did." They were both laughing, although Josef would have rather called it 'giggling madly'. It was early in the morning and there weren't many people moving in and out of the building at this hour. Even so, he had a slight notion in the back of his mind that if anyone walked in on them at that moment, they would have thought both him and Phoebe mad.

Once their giggling died down, Phoebe squeezed his hand back, before releasing it and rubbing the pads of her fingers together.

"You know, if you want to go out still, we can." Josef returned his glasses to his nose and smiled at her as she blushed. "It won't be a date, but you can meet my best friend and sister, Vanja. There's this great café near here where we always hang out. It's called Déjà Brew."

Her blush didn't die down, but a smile returned to her face. "I'd like that."

"Great, see you there, gold-horns." He turned on his heel and made his way towards the elevator. He smiled when he heard the little squeal of delight coming from the front desk.

***

Mr Young had two offices, one in the Behemoth tower where he spent the majority of his time. It was his office for the new hires, people who weren't allowed to move between the main building and the hallways belowground.

His second office was situated within the roots of the facility, where only employees with the correct level clearance were allowed to visit him. Josef had the right level of clearance, courtesy of Phoebe the day before. She had printed him out a new Senior Caretaker ID before he even knew he was fully promoted. Uncle Josef would have been proud of him, he was sure of that.

He stepped into Mr Young's lower office following a polite knock and a calm response of "Enter." That early in the morning, Josef knew he wouldn't find Mr Young in the Behemoth. And yet he felt as if he had stepped into a slightly darker version of his office up top. Both had linoleum floors, minimal decoration, and mahogany desks presented in the very centre of the circular room. There were no windows here, but the chandelier hanging from the ceiling gave off a bright, white glow, and Josef was grateful that he always wore his dark glasses.

There was something that resembled a mural on his left, a stone relief featuring Young's ancestor, Sir Thaddeus. It was identical to the one in his other office but was lit up with wall-mounted spotlights from up above. Sir Thaddeus was a handsome, kingly man, with gentle blueish-violet eyes. His hair was somewhere between chestnut brown and dirty blond, falling across a broad forehead. He was clean-shaven, with red lips below a flat, broad nose.

Mr Young was at his desk, writing something, and didn't even look up when Josef came in. So Josef waited, familiarising himself with the office from where he stood in the doorway.

"Close the door, Mr Ryan."

Josef jumped and did as told, shutting the door with a click that sounded far too loud. Mr Young still refused to look up. Josef wandered closer, shuffling his feet. In the corner of the room (or what functioned as a corner), situated behind Mr Young, Josef spied a dog bed, and upon it, a furry creature. The creature had chestnut brown fur and appeared to be the size of a human, maybe slightly shorter than him. It had its back to him and Mr Young, and Josef imagined that it was sleeping.

"Mr Ryan, what brings you here." Mr Young still didn't look up at him, and his words were more of a demand than a question.

"Oh, um." Josef cleared his throat. "I just wanted to make sure that my timetable was correct, sir. There have been a lot of changes recently, and … " He was cut off, Mr Young bringing his hand up to silence him. In the corner of the room, the furred creature stirred.

"Your current timetable is correct. You will be aiding the other Senior Caretakers in preparing the halcyon chicks from last winter for release. Then you are free to go home." Mr Young finally looked up at him, but Josef was no longer paying attention as he smiled disarmingly. "But don't worry, Mr Ryan. You will be paid the full rate you are owed, and on Wednesday, you will be back to your regular timetable, from 6:00 a.m. to 6:00 p.m."

The creature behind Mr Young had shifted, twisted around atop its bed so that it could face them. It was a humanoid rabbit, Josef realised, with the flat, pinkish nose, the three lips, and long ears hidden beneath a head full of brown curls. Its eyes were massive, with wide, round pupils and brown irises that were so dark they almost looked black. The eye whites were but slivers at the edges. Josef noticed that it was holding its arms close to its chest and that its breathing was laboured and thin.

He made a move to step towards it, but Mr Young thrust his hand out to stop him. "Where do you think you're going, Mr Ryan?"

Josef didn't know where his voice went when those purple eyes penetrated straight through him.

"To help," he squeaked. "It's hurt."

"Darling had an accident. He was already looked at, and the vet decided that he simply needs to rest."

Josef was convinced. After all, would Mr Young lie to him? Could eyes so beautiful be capable of lying? His head felt fuzzy, and the more he looked into the depths of Young's eyes, the more he was starting to forget what he came here for. Why was he arguing with his boss in the first place? Maybe he should step back, maybe go ask Phoebe for a painkiller. He was starting to get a migraine again.

He said his goodbyes to Mr Young and, with one last look at Darling, left the office.

The farther away he got from Young's office, the more his headache seemed to recede. The fuzzy spots in the corners of his vision slowly melted away, and yet Josef was still struggling to remember the conversation. His mind began to wander as he meandered through the halls of the FCMC.

Josef remembered only snippets of his childhood. His parents were often at work, and his uncles were busy despite working from home. But there were moments that he remembered vividly. Sitting on his father's lap, listening to ancient dragon bedtime stories, curled atop his stomach that glowed like burning coals. The days where his mother would take him out into the backyard, teach him how to shoot a bow. Before his birth she had been an Olympic-level athlete. Her arms were almost as thick as Dante's, her fingers were covered in callouses, her hair was cropped short at her chin, and her cheek was marred by a horrid scar from her training days. She was the most beautiful creature young Sef had ever seen.

"Strength, Josef," she used to say, "is not a substitute for kindness. Without strength, a kind man cannot change the world. Without kindness, a strong man does not want to change the world. A man who is both strong and kind, he will know how to change the world, even if it's just to change the world for one person."

Josef could overpower Mr Young; how could a scrawny human ever measure up to him with his years of weightlifting and his dragon might? But he didn't, not in that moment. He didn't, and couldn't, help Darling. He couldn't be kind and compassionate to that creature that looked at him with sad, forlorn eyes. What good was his human compassion if he couldn't act upon it?

Josef remembered how his uncles would sometimes sit around the fireplace, simply talking. Uncle Josef would tell him about all the animals he worked with, from the smallest of mischievous pixies to the colossal, sea-faring leviathans. Uncle Brooke would smile, and the fondness within that smile always stuck with him. Uncle Brooke, like Elspeth, seemed wise beyond his years to his favourite nephew.

"Firecracker," he used to say, "why are you sad?"

"Because those people were mean to you and Uncle Josef."

Uncle Brooke would smile, picking little Sef up. "Don't be sad for me, firecracker. Be sad for them."

"But why, Uncle Brooke?"

"Because they are sad people. Happy people do not hurt others. Happy people do not act rude or mean towards others. Sad people do that, and those sad people deserve our compassion." Uncle Brooke had a crooked nose and two large front teeth, he had thin lips and squinty eyes, and he had a smile that Josef believed could scare away the mightiest of storms. "Be kind to others, Josef. Be kind, because there are sad people in the world who do not understand kindness. Be the one to teach them how to be kind."

I failed you, Josef thought. *I cannot be strong right now. I want to be kind, but I cannot. Something is stopping me.*

His headache returned, but his head had never felt clearer. He took a deep breath, standing before the doors of the elevator, and began to replay the interaction within the office again. Every time, he came back to Darling's crossed arms. His breathing was shallow, his ribs had been broken. He wouldn't have wanted to hold himself where it hurt the most.

And then it struck him; the rabbit had something within his grip. And he was looking right at Josef, maintaining constant, unbreaking eye contact.

11

BARISTA GUY AND RECEPTIONIST GIRL

After hours, Josef decided to approach Phoebe.

"Are we off, then?" she asked, already packing up her bag.

"Yes, I suppose so." He swiped them both out, returning the ID card to Phoebe but keeping his in hand, playing around with it. "Can I ask you something?"

"Anything. We're friends after all, right?" Her smile was disarming.

"I made friends with Vanja the first day we met, so I'd say we are."

"What did you want to ask me?"

"Does Mr Young have any pets?"

Phoebe stopped, her red backpack hanging in her loose grip. Now that he could see her fully, not hidden behind her desk, he thought of her as very beautiful. She was slightly fat and a bit curvy. She was dressed in a pencil skirt and a suit jacket, both of them the same shade of red, that accentuated her round figure perfectly. The blonde hair atop her head was matched by the striking shade of gold on her furry legs, and her hooves were decorated by red ribbons that almost reminded Josef of the straps of sandals. If he was attracted to women, he very well would have gone out with her.

"He has a rabbit. Flemish giant; big, fluffy bugger who's called Darling and lives in his office." She was eyeing him. He didn't really understand what that look meant, but he came closer to her and whispered in her ear.

"Does he have a human form?"

Phoebe jumped back from him as if he had shocked her. Her eyes flew wildly around the lobby, her ears twitching slightly despite them being perfectly human-looking. She made a zipping motion over her mouth, and he handed her a slip of paper he had previously prepared.

"Your number?"

"And address. We'll talk about this some other time."

She nodded, and when he smiled at her, she smiled back. Arm in arm, they exited the lobby, climbed into her red car, and zoomed off.

***

Josef was the first one out of the car. He manoeuvred his way around to the other side, opening the door for Phoebe as his gaze wandered. It landed on the table taken up by Vanja, dressed now completely in her goth outfit from five years ago, and a dark-haired, bearded person wearing makeup twice as heavy as hers and a shirt that showed even more of their ample cleavage than Vanja's usually did. Josef never thought he would see the day where one of Vanja's partners managed to out-goth her, not Oh Great Vanja herself.

"Rus, hey!" he called out to her, and the rusałka turned her head with a flip of her long locks. *What a show off*, Josef thought to himself, *a damn endearing one, unfortunately.*

Vanja and her new partner both stood up when he and Phoebe walked up. The new person wore golden contact lenses and had Doc Martens that reached their knees, with leg braces made of black leather and a dark type of metal caging in their legs.

"I like your shoes." Josef smiled.

The new person smiled back, and Josef felt pleased with himself. "Thank you. I'm Murphy, by the way, Vanja's boyfriend."

Then it clicked for him, just as he was taking Murphy's hand. "Hey, you're the new barista guy!"

Vanja was cackling at his side, and Murphy was trying to hold her up when her knees buckled.

"Yup. I'm way tamer in my work clothes." Murphy had perfect white teeth, surrounded by deep red lips framed by his carefully styled facial hair. He had dark brown hair and skin that was naturally tan, paired with a wide, flat nose. He looked like no one that Josef knew, and yet something about him seemed so oddly familiar.

"I almost didn't recognise you in all of that makeup." From behind Josef, Phoebe was standing with her hands behind her back, awkwardly looking between him, Vanja, and Murphy. Her tone of voice wasn't unkind; however, something told Josef that she didn't mean it as a compliment.

"Phoebe Oikonomou, I never thought I would see you again." The hiss of contempt that Murphy let out took even Vanja by surprise, if her open-mouthed expression was anything to go by. "Still working for that cunt, are you?"

"Murphy!"

Phoebe was seething, Josef could feel it from where she stood at his back. "I have no choice, you Mean Girl-ass bitch!"

"Phoebe, that's enough." He could feel the tension rising, he could feel it like he could feel the heat of the sun beating down upon his face. Phoebe was still behind him, as if using him as a shield. Or a fence, to stop herself from making the wrong move. He wasn't sure which was worse.

Murphy was holding onto Vanja with both hands, shaking from top to bottom. His features were melting, twisting and shifting. His left eye was pinched inwards, and his right arm was undulating weirdly as it visibly shortened.

Then they both threw their hands up into the air and left, Phoebe disappearing into her red car again and Murphy limping, with one leg shorter than the other, towards his black motorbike. Josef and Vanja were left alone, standing on either side of their favourite table at Déjà Brew.

"Takeout?"

"Absolutely."

***

"I'm gonna go broke if I have to buy three puppuccinos every time I get out of the house." Josef took out an earbud just in time to hear a loud, wet gulp that came from Spot's direction. Vanja giggled against him, laying atop him on his sofa, her head pillowed on top of his stomach.

"She's happy, can you blame her?"

"I guess I can't." They fell into a comfortable silence again, him listening to music on his phone while Vanja was busy reading a book. From where he lay, he couldn't quite read what it was, but he knew for a fact it wasn't English, German, or Italian. It did, however, feature a haygriff on the front cover, the leporine cousin of the griffon and hippogriff. It had the back end of a ptarmigan, with its rabbit-like paws, and the front end of a snow hare, long ears and all.

"What do you think that was about?" he asked her after she had leafed through five more pages. Her bookmark was a feather shaped out of metal, made by Uncle Brooke for her thirtieth birthday. She slotted it into her book and set the book down, turning so that she was laying on her stomach, her chin digging slightly into Josef's belly.

"I think Phoebe and Murphy are exes," she said bluntly.

"Did he tell you that?"

"No, he has not texted me yet."

Josef scratched the side of his face, his glasses forgotten somewhere on the coffee table. "How much do you know about him?"

"Well, he is Murphy Young, age thirty-nine, goth since age thirteen. He work at Déjà Brew, but he prefer photography and modelling. He has website where he post his photographs, they are very good. He is … "

"His name is Murphy Young?"

"Yes? It common name, is it not?"

"What colour are his natural eyes?"

Vanja gave him a little pout before she put on her thinking face again. "Purple. Very pretty colour, I wanted to make painting of his eyes, but we are both so busy that I haven't finished it."

"He's related to Charles Young?"

"Maybe? If he is Young, and his eyes are purple, does it mean he is definitely family to your boss?"

Josef paused, resting his hand atop Vanja's head. Her eyes fluttered shut, and she snuggled deeper into his gut, chasing down the warmth of his dragon fire.

"He reminds me of Young, that's the problem. And I saw his eyes before, they're the same shade."

"He look nothing like Young beside eyes."

"No, but something in his face reminds me of my boss."

Vanja opened her eyes again, trailing them across the living room. "We can ask him. Murphy is so kind, he tell me everything I ask of him. We have no secrets. He know I am part rusałka, and my mother ran off with selkie man to have my sister, abandoning me in England. He know your family took care of me when I was searching for my father. He know how much you mean to me, he would tell you everything, if just to make me happy."

"Thank you, Vanja. Tell me, what was that about his body going all … "

"Melty."

"Yes."

"Ah, Murphy is shapeshifter."

"Oh, really? Huh, that's exactly like Shark."

"Your boyfriend." Her cheeky, sharp-toothed smirk was pissing him off.

"No! Not my … Vanja! I can't date someone who is being held captive in a facility for non-sentient magical animals!"

"You have to do something about that."

Maybe the sigh he let out was overly dramatic, but he didn't really care. "But what? What can I do? I wasn't even allowed to see them today."

"Don't know. Talk to Murphy. Talk to Phoebe. Maybe Murphy knows. Phoebe might know, she work there. And when you have plan, I will help you."

"Thank you for your wealth of wisdom."

"I, Oh Great Vanja, am pleased with your thank you."

12

---·---

WHEN KNOWLEDGE IS POWER

Phoebe met him at the front desk the next time he came into work. She was, as always, dressed in an all-red get-up, but her golden accents seemed more toned down that day. She still gave him a smile, although it was no longer the beaming, bright thing from before when she still crushed on him.

"Dragon-eyes, hey."

The ID scanner beeped loudly when Josef scanned himself in. Phoebe's lithe fingers were click-clacking over her keyboard, and she wasn't paying as much attention to him as she used to.

"Are you alright? What happened two days ago was … "

She cut him off, snapping her head around sharply. "It's not your fault, Brooke, but I'd rather not talk about it." She turned back to the computer, and he could hear her chewing on something as he thought.

"Would you tell me where you knew Murphy from, or does that count under 'it'?"

"We used to be best friends, college roommates," she said after a moment of silence. "We fell out because I was offered a job here, at his uncle's company, some six years ago. It was either that or having to move back to Greece to live with my parents." Josef hummed as he listened, and Phoebe's ears were twitching again with each new note.

"I didn't know you were Greek."

A grin brightened up her face, and she turned to look at him again with those shining eyes of hers. "Of course not. I grew up in the UK, living with my auntie. But finding satyrs outside of Greece is kind of hard, no? We are indigenous to that part of Europe."

He was nodding along, and with each nod his glasses slipped further down his nose, until he was scrambling to catch them in mid-air. That got a laugh out of Phoebe, and Josef felt compelled to join in with her. He was, deep down, annoyed that she wouldn't tell him more, but that little spark of anger was overshadowed by his joy at seeing her happy, at knowing that they would be alright after all.

"Would you like to go see a movie with me tomorrow? As friends, no Vanja or Murphy, just the two of us."

Phoebe had the sort of smile that could light up a ballroom, and she gave him such a smile right then. "I would love to, dragon-eyes. How about that new superhero movie? The one with the underwater kingdom."

"Great, it's decided! See you then."

"Bye!"

***

He got in touch with Murphy through Vanja a week and a half later. He debated with himself (and with Spot) whether it was rude to text a complete stranger without said stranger even knowing that he had their number. In the end, he was the one being invited to the complete stranger's apartment, so he supposed that it evened out.

"Make yourself at home, Brooke." Murphy waved his arm out in an arc, presenting to Josef his very clean, and yet very cluttered, apartment. Josef smiled and stepped in, thinking how Murphy must have picked up the 'Brooke' thing from Vanja.

"Thanks, I appreciate you inviting me over."

Murphy was milling around, a cat with two tails trailing in his wake. "Of course! You're, what, Vanja's brother, right? Even if not biological. It would be weird if I purposefully tried ruining our relationship. I want to be friends with my future brother-in-law."

Josef's eyes snapped up from the nekomata that was making biscuits on the blanket-covered sofa and zeroed in on Murphy. Here, within his own home, Murphy was dressed far more casually. His makeup was toned down, although he still wore black mascara, and his lips were a dark shade of burgundy. He wore an oversized hoodie with the logo of a band Josef didn't recognise, and a pair of jeans, both of which gave him a much more masculine silhouette than in the coffee shop. His hair was still styled the same way, and his facial hair was still immaculately groomed.

"Whoa there, brother-in-law? Haven't you and Vanja been dating for, what ... "

"Two months. And don't sweat it, Brooke! I don't even have a ring! I'm just thinking ahead." The nekomata meowed in protest when it was scooped up, only to immediately settle back down when Murphy placed it in his lap.

"Murphy, man, Vanja's never been with anyone for longer than half a year, what makes you think you'll last that long?" The sofa was covered in a thin layer of cat fur, and both of the armrests were covered up by photography gear, yet Josef managed to squeeze himself in next to Murphy, sitting shoulder-to-shoulder with him, both of them gently petting the two-tailed cat.

"Because she told me." His voice dropped an octave, and he stared right at Josef. In that moment, without the golden contacts, Murphy's eyes were so brilliantly purple that they didn't seem real. The shape of those eyes, too, was the exact same almond shape as Charles Young's.

"She told you what?" Josef had to fight the lump in his throat and mentally scream at himself not to just ask Murphy, then and there, about his uncle.

"That she never felt like anyone truly understood her. Except for me. Because I understand what it's ... what it feels like to be estranged from your family, to feel other in a country you weren't born in, and to always look for that one person that understands, never to find them." Those purple eyes were covered in a sheen of tears, and Josef moved to wrap his arms around Murphy on instinct. He wasn't sure how long they sat there, him just holding onto Murphy as the other wept. He didn't know when he himself started crying, and when his tears twisted within him into full-out sobs. At some point, Murphy was hugging him back, trying to wrap his short arms around Josef's broad back, lending a bony shoulder for him to cry into.

"Your uncle," Josef began, and he could feel Murphy's body tensing, "is holding someone within his facility that understands me in a way you and Vanja understand each other."

"I'll help you."

Josef immediately pulled back, although he didn't dislodge Murphy's hands that still rested on the small of his back. It was comforting, it felt safe, and he needed that safety.

"I don't want your help, Murphy. I can't ask that of you. Just ... tell me everything that you're able to about your uncle."

The nekomata danced and leapt from Murphy's lap to his just as its owner was getting up. Murphy paced, and he paced a lot. All day, for hours as Josef listened to him talk, Murphy paced. He wore braces upon his legs even indoors, metallic cages that made his legs rigid, caused him to limp. And yet he walked, and paced, and jumped around the room with every burst of emotion, even when it began to hurt.

And this is what Josef learned from him: Charles Young was one of the oldest shapeshifters in existence. No one knew his true face, his true age, or where he even hailed from. He was a direct descendant of Sir Thaddeus the Dragon Friend, but no one knew when the shapeshifting gene was introduced into their blood. Murphy always wondered if such a perfect replication of human and animal genes alike was even native to Earth in the first place. Young was no werebeast, skinchanger, or nymph, capable of shifting only between one human and one animal form, much like Shark.

Charles Young was a greedy man. He used his ancestor's good name to start up a company that made him rich, while everyone outside of the Young family saw him as a philanthropist, an altruist. The FCMC, in all its glory up Above, was made with only money in mind down Beneath.

A good ten, maybe fifteen years ago, Murphy's uncle showed up to a family gathering with a new face. A dimpled chin, round lips as red as blood, skin as pale as snow, and hair as dark as a black hole. That's when things stopped adding up. That was when the energy bills stopped being paid, but no energy company could safely say that Young was partnered up with them. Murphy had been the black sheep of his family ever since he came out to his parents as genderfluid, but not even his homophobic, Bible-thumping aunt could say that she hated Murphy more than she hated Charles. And the family dug. They dug deep.

"More security?"

"So much more." Murphy was taking a sip of gin and still pacing, seemingly uncaring that he had work tomorrow. "Too much for a simple veterinary practice, unless that's not all that the FCMC is. Have you ever seen hundreds of guards working at a zoo?"

"No, and I worked at two zoos in uni." Josef was nursing a whiskey with C oke, Hissitis the nekomata (named that because she was a very hissy kitten, apparently) rubbing up against his leg as he pet her fuzzy head.

"My family also dug up proof that Charles was constantly employing and then firing different animal behaviourists, trainers, et cetera. People who knew how to discipline creatures, more or less."

Through the fuzz of the whiskey, Josef was putting all this information together. Slowly, the puzzle pieces were beginning to fit. "I'm a trainer. My uncle trained hellhounds and I did an apprenticeship under him almost twenty years ago."

"And that's why you got to meet … "

"That's why I met Shark. Cause I could discipline them. So Young could control them better." The whiskey was discarded upon a stack of books that functioned as a coffee table. Josef stuffed his face into Hissitis' fluffy belly, feeling the gentle rumbling from her purrs. Curse his dragon genes, he was such a lightweight.

Murphy finished off his gin and reached over for Josef's discarded whiskey, clearly assuming that the man wasn't planning on finishing it. "And now, Charles has probably figured out that you became friends with his super powerful alien-cum-power generator, and will restrict your access to them as much as he is able to."

"Why's he not just fire me, then?"

"Because you're the only Braun left, Brooke. The only one who has your uncle's knowledge. The only one Charles can still manipulate to do his bidding." Murphy seemed to want to leave it at that, and Josef was almost ready to let him. But then there was the question:

"How do I get Shark out?"

"I don't know," Murphy said with too much honesty for Josef's taste. "That's for you to figure out."

13

—·—

WHEN POWER IS CORRUPTION

It was a few weeks before Josef was allowed to see Shark again. It was disconcerting for him, and he found himself bunking with Vanja more often. Nightmares of Shark's bruised and bloodied corpse haunted his dreams, with images of his father's dry husk spliced in every few nights.

The one positive of his off days was the ability to come up with a plan. Neither Phoebe nor Murphy knew why Shark was being kept at the facility, barring the obvious energy source. Neither knew how to free them exactly, but the fact that Phoebe was willing to talk to him about it was a start.

"I'd love to help out, Brooke," she said during one of their café excursions, "but I don't have anywhere else to go. If Mr Young finds out I helped you, or if freeing Shark makes the FCMC collapse, I have nowhere else to go."

Josef was chewing the end of a croissant, his glasses perched at the very tip of his nose. "Not even Greece?"

"I'm not going back to Greece." And that was the end of the conversation that day.

It took him another two weeks to get the information out of her, although reluctantly on her part.

Vanja was there, playing tug with Spot in Josef's living room while he and Phoebe were on his sofa playing a game of chess. He didn't quite remember how the conversation started, but it ended with Phoebe spilling her heart out:

"They want to marry me off," she sobbed, and her king tumbled off the playing board. "To some billy twice my age, so that he can teach me how to be a 'proper woman'." Maybe it was Vanja's presence that finally did it, maybe it was the cosiness of a shared dinner and warm blankets for the three of them to hide under. Something finally made Phoebe crack, and Josef's heart broke for her.

"You are proper woman, no?" Vanja approached her with a cup of hot chocolate, and Spot nosed at her knee.

"I'm too autistic, apparently. They sent me to live here in England with my aunt, but she's not much better than me."

Josef wrapped an arm around her, piling another blanket around her shaking shoulders.

"I can't return there, I can't!"

The day ended with them curled underneath a blanket fort, empty mugs discarded across the floor. Josef lay upon his back, Phoebe and Vanja curled up on either side of him within the crooks of his arms, their heads weighing down his chest. He fell asleep last, listening to the cars outside of his window and watching the starless sky yawning endlessly at him.

***

He got to visit Shark on a Monday, when Phoebe welcomed him at the front desk and told him that he was needed down below again. He went immediately.

The penetrating cold from the rooms Beneath fought against his naturally high body temperature. The room he usually met with Shark in was empty, so he followed the whispers of ice crystals and cold air until he came upon a room dominated by screaming and roaring.

Within the centre of it sat a large pillar, sparkling arcs of electricity dancing around it madly. Shark was in the corner of the room, behind another set of bars, a collar wrapped tightly around their neck and their face melting and moulding into that of a black-furred panther.

"Enough! Get out of here!"

The guards within the room, two of them exactly, dropped their batons and their poles, slamming the door shut behind them as they went. Josef's voice echoed off the walls of the small room, barely audible above the sparking of the generator. There was a gate left swinging open in the centre of the room.

"So, this is what Mr Young keeps you here for?"

Shark's face collapsed in on itself, before reforming into their usual handsome, yet gaunt, features. "Yes. I'm an energy source. Without me to power this building, Young would have no hope in controlling all the beasts he sells and butchers. I make him money, and make sure the other things he makes money off of don't escape. And as long as Young has my name, I am his to do with as he pleases." A heavy pause hung in the air between them. "You left me, Brooke." It was as if one of the ice crystals from the air had been shot at him, piercing him through the heart.

"I didn't mean to," he begged and took a step towards the gate. "I wasn't allowed back here." Shark took a step in tandem, meeting him halfway. It was the first time they were allowed to touch each other without the bars, without the eyes of other people upon them. Shark's arms wrapped tightly around Josef's neck, and his arms went to the small of their back.

"Show me that you didn't mean it, my love."

So he did, despite the crackling of the generator that drowned out their words and despite the collar that wrapped around Shark's throat until their skin went purple. He touched them and caressed them and spent all the time he could proving to them just how much he had missed them.

***

They lay on Shark's side of the room, with the gate swinging freely upon its hinges, touching each other as much as they wanted to. Shark's arm was thrown across Josef's stomach, and Josef was pressing kisses against their neck with such fervour, as if it was as necessary to him as breathing.

"Do you really think this is love?" Josef breathed into the crook of their neck. It wasn't the question he wanted to ask, but it was the only one that felt right in that moment.

"It's a feeling," Shark rested their lips against the crown of Josef's head. "And love is also a feeling. Does it have to be love, this early on? Can it not just be a connection, maybe one borne of lust? The want of another warm body against yours, bringing you pleasure?"

Josef trailed a kiss up their long, sinewy neck, until he reached their lips. "Would you mind if it ended up being love at some point?"

"No," they said, kissing him back, "I wouldn't. I like you. Your kindness when we first met. I like your beautiful eyes. I like how perfectly imperfect you are. I like that you're not scared of me, that you don't see me as something to study, something other. I like that you stayed. I'm sorry for influencing you." Their lips brushed against his again, and Josef tightened his arm around their waist.

"I'm other too. I don't fit in, not as much as I'd like to. I guess I didn't fight against the mind control all that much because of it. Because I was lonely too."

"And I love you for that. And for the fact that you stayed and came back for me."

Josef pulled back and stared deep into the depths of Shark's eyes. He saw the galaxies swirling in a vortex of fantastical colours, like a pot full of different coloured paint as it is being stirred for the first time.

"I'll get you out of here, *mi tesoro*."

INTERLUDE 4: TIME FALLS

Darling rarely kept track of time. Each day felt identical within the confines of Young's office. It harkened back to the days when he was still a kit, unaware yet of the wider world, living each day as if it was to be his last. The forest had a day and night cycle, and the four seasons left him with a reminder of how many years had passed, but weeks and months meant nothing to him. The birds didn't need to sing of Mondays, and the foxes didn't understand the concept of weekends. The rushing river didn't know that it froze over in January, and the trees weren't aware that they lost their leaves in September.

Each day that he spent curled up around the recorder atop his bed, stuck within Young's office, all he could do was think. He wasn't taken out, he couldn't shift, his ribs were still healing. And the days stretched out longer and longer, and the recorder was forever cold against his skin.

Then, one day, Brooke arrived again. The last time he had seen the man in the glasses, there was no recognition within his russet eyes. This time, Brooke purposefully dipped down his glasses and gazed at Darling with pity.

"Mr Ryan, what brings you here?" Young was at his desk as always, busy with paperwork that Darling couldn't read. There were notes scattered around the tabletop, reminders that couldn't quite replace his lost recorder.

"Mr Young," Brooke began, and his voice was a deep, pleasant rumble, and Darling could, just for a moment, imagine perfectly why Shark loved this human so much. "I want to bring to your attention that your ... how do I say this?"

Young waited, and Brooke fumbled, and Darling wished he could speak up in a language they would both understand.

"Mr Young," Brooke began again, "you must free Shark." The air grew still within the room. Darling wasn't able to see Young's expression, but he commended Brooke for holding his gaze for so long, letting the tension grow with each passing second.

The little clock upon Young's desk ticked away. Darling's heartbeat fell in line with its tune.

"My dear Mr Ryan," Young finally said, his words slow and elongated, "I know that Subject-20-465 seems sympathetic, but we are keeping them here for their own good."

Darling watched as Brooke's resolve crumbled, as his hands began to shake and his shoulders fell forward.

He wanted to say something, he was opening his mouth and about to speak, when the walkie-talkie upon Young's desk interrupted him. Young barely used it, and when it clicked awake Darling jumped in his skin.

"Boss, need you on level +5, ASAP." It clicked off again, and Young excused himself, leaving him and Brooke alone. They stood there like that for what felt like hours, neither wishing to move, neither wanting to break the silence and the stillness.

Brooke's eyes were on him, and Darling had to wonder how much Shark had told him, how much he truly knew and was willing to do to free them.

That was when his phone rang. He picked it up with what amounted to a smile.

"Hello? How can I help you? Hmm? Yes, I'm Josef Brooke Ryan, who's calling? My father? Is everything alright with him? He's ... but are you sure? I called him last night and he was still walking and doing fine! A stroke ... I understand. Yes, I ... How long does he have left? Oh. Oh. Alright. I'll be there tomorrow. Yes, that's fine. I'll stay with him however long it takes. Thank you for letting me know. What's your name again? M'kay, thank you for the information, Sue. I'm glad someone like you is taking care of him. Thank you again. Goodbye."

With each word he spoke, Brooke's face fell, and his voice hardened. With each beat of silence that followed, his demeanour crumbled, until he was sobbing into his hands. He didn't even wait for Young to return, he simply left.

Darling realised then that he was alone. Utterly and completely alone. As in the days of the forest, when it was just him against the world, he was completely alone. Brooke, his father clearly on his deathbed, wouldn't help them after all.

When Young returned to his office sometime later, Darling lay with his back to the door, the recorder pressed against his bare skin. He listened as the man wandered around his office, mumbling and muttering to himself as he went. He paid no mind to Darling, and Darling was fine with that.

He just waited. The passage of time meant little to him, but he knew when the sun rose and set. So he waited. Until night fell.

14

— • —

THE END OF THE UNIVERSE

"Are you sure about this, Brooke?" Murphy was driving the car, a black Kia that didn't attract attention. From the back seat, sitting next to a napping Spot, Josef was staring up at the starless sky, his glasses put away in his coat pocket to let him see better.

"I'm sure, now drive."

Vanja looked back at him from the passenger seat, her eyebrows downturned and her lips pulled into a pout. He hoped he hadn't sounded rude.

"But what about plan, Brooke?" she asked, still looking at him.

"I'm sorry, Rus, but we don't have time for that." Murphy had switched the radio off some time ago, and Josef bemoaned the lack of music to distract himself.

"We'll just ... improvise," Murphy added, his voice wavering.

"We will. And at least Phoebe promised to help us," Josef said as the car pulled up outside the FCMC building.

She met them right at the entrance, wearing a muted red suit in such stark contrast to her usual attire. She looked scared, worrying away at her bottom lip, refusing to meet his or Vanja's eyes.

"Where's Murphy?"

"He's staying in the car with Spot."

Her expression didn't change, but she reached out to grasp his hands. "Think this through, Brooke. Are you sure you want to do this?"

"You don't have to help," Vanja cut in, getting in between Phoebe and Josef. All three of them were buzzing with energy, and the tension in the air was palpable.

"I dismissed the guards. The building is empty. I'm coming with you." Phoebe reached out and grasped Vanja's hand. She was still holding onto Josef with the other.

"You have this much power?"

"No, I just know how to hack the company's systems."

"Girls, later." Josef extracted himself from Phoebe's grasp and began making his way towards the elevator. Phoebe and Vanja, still holding hands, trailed behind him. Their eyes were on the back of his head, boring into him, tracing every one of his steps as he navigated the empty space of the Behemoth's ground floor. The waning light of the moon filtered through the glass windows, creating scattered crystal-like lights across the floor and walls.

The elevator ride was silent, the creaking and gasping of the mechanisms reverberating in Josef's ears. The lower they went, the less light there was.

"I lead now." Vanja's voice was barely a whisper, a breath against the back of his neck as her slim, fluid body brushed past his elbow. Her eyes, so pale up Above, seemed almost biolumi-nescent in the guts of the Behemoth. Josef felt Phoebe's much shorter body press against his side, the faint clip-clopping of her hooves the only sound audible within the penetrating darkness of the Beneath.

"Follow the cold air."

The silence was horrifying. The buzz of the electric lights, the distant cacophony of scientists working, the marching of the guards, all were gone. The cold, metal walls beneath his fingers were still; they forgot to vibrate now that only a fraction of the usual population of the Beneath existed. Josef wanted to pull his hand away, wanted to exist without touch, without sound, suspended within the darkness. The simple action of brushing his fingers against a bruise in the wall's shell was overwhelming, shooting electricity through his entire body. But he had to hold onto something, he had to know where he was going. He still existed, even if the world no longer did. The universe could have ended outside, and he never would have known that he was the only thing left alive.

"Brooke, talk to me." Phoebe's lips were pressed to his shoul-der, the highest place on him she could reach. Her quiet, vaguely accented voice sent a shiver down his back, and the golden hoop earrings she had worn since his first day at work were sparkling faintly in the corner of his eye.

"I'm here, Phoebe, I'm here."

Her hand was pressed into the side of his stomach, her hooves were still clacking against the metal floor of the passageway, her breath was tickling his neck. Vanja was up ahead, and she was turning around now, every so often, her pale blue eyes the only point of light within the consuming darkness.

And then Josef felt a soft, warm hand wrap around his wrist. He felt fur lining the palm, and the thumb was placed lower on his wrist than he would have expected, gentle pinpricks from claws digging into his skin.

"Darling."

"What? Who? Brooke, there other person here?" Vanja asked, her head swivelling around wildly.

"It's Darling. He's Shark's friend." The warm palm travelled up his arm, from his wrist to his bicep, until it rested upon his shoulder. With the combined pressure of Darling and Phoebe's bodies against him, Josef felt real again. He felt alive again.

"It's getting very cold. We must be on the right track," Phoebe muttered, and Josef wondered if her words were meant for the rest of them or not. Darling let out a chittering tooth grind, what Josef assumed to be in agreement.

"This door, yes? Generator?" Vanja's trilling accent reached Josef through the darkness again. There was silence from the other side.

He went in, Darling close on his heels. The lightning that danced in arcs around the generator lit the room up blue. The contorting shadows on the walls almost reminded him of the reflection of water seen through a sheet of glass. They undulated, gyrated, melting into each other and then falling apart like scorned lovers.

There, lit up by the blue light, their eyes reflecting each galloping bolt that raced through the air, was Shark.

"I knew you would both come for me." Shark's smile was pressed against the bars of their cage. Darling rushed past Josef, throwing himself at Shark. He wore only a shirt multiple sizes too small, his hands trembling as he passed a small, black recorder over to Shark.

"Thlayli, you clever, clever thing!" Shark was looking at Darling ... at Thlayli with so much admiration. Josef forced himself to stop. He had moved up to the doors of the cage, pressing his lips against the lock and blowing bursts of hot air over it, puffing and huffing until the lock began to glow red. And he stopped himself, right as the metal reached its melting point, to watch Shark and Thlayli. Shark's arms were stuck through the bars, grasping at the short fur on Thlayli's back. The rabbit man was holding gently onto Shark's head that rested against his shoulder. Seconds passed, and they weren't separating; minutes passed, and Josef noticed that Shark had started crying. Thlayli's eyes didn't water, but he looked distressed with his blown-wide eyes, his perked, rigid ears, and the way his fur stood on end across his entire body.

Finally, they separated, and Shark reached for the record er."*I'll make sure Welei never touches you again. You're mine, Darling. Mine!*"

The voice reverberated through the small room, drowning out the crackling and spitting of the generator. Although only for a moment, as the generator began to whir louder. The lightning became more frantic, more wild. It sparked and danced, and it shot out, hitting the walls, the floor, the ceiling. Josef threw himself at Thlayli, pressing him against the bars of Welei's cage. A bolt shot past Josef's cheek, lighting up the terrified look upon Thlayli's face. Another bolt struck him in the back between his shoulder blades. He felt the underdeveloped muscles of his wings clench and constrict; his coat and shirt burned away, and the stench of burned flesh filled the room. The generator grew brighter, whiter, the arcs transforming finally into a singular bolt. With a deafening crack it shattered the door of the cage, and a moment later, the entire thing collapsed in on itself. Bits of metal pelted Josef's exposed back.

"Brooke, Thlayli, are you alright?" Welei's voice was frantic, their lithe body shooting through the door and over to them both. Thlayli was terrified but unharmed, and he threw himself at Welei the moment he was free from Josef's grasp. His dragon genes were strong, but Josef still felt the pulsing ache in his back. The wound burned and pinched as he shed himself of his coat and shirt. The shirt he threw over Thlayli, covering the tiny garment he had most likely stolen from Young. The light orange button-up reached to just above the middle of his thighs, and the sleeves reached to his wrists. The coat he wrapped around Welei's much smaller frame, buttoning it up to the very neck to hide the hideous hole in their throat that the collar had left.

"My hero." Welei's hands were immediately on Josef's bare skin, tracing across a pair of scars beneath his pectorals, then down to a set of claw marks on his side, reaching back upwards to wrap their arms around his neck. They pressed a kiss to another scar on his shoulder, their gentle hands brushing over the burn on his back. They kissed him, and the burn cooled in seconds beneath their touch.

"I love you, *mi tesoro*. Welei."

They smiled with a mouth full of shark teeth, and it seemed like the most beautiful thing Josef had ever seen. "I want you to say my name again, Brooke. I want you to own it, willingly. Say it again."

"Welei."

"Who do you think you are, Braun's nephew? Stealing my pets from right under my nose!"

15

— · —

STRENGTH WITHOUT KINDNESS PROVES NOTHING

Josef had scooped Welei up into his arms. Vanja and Phoebe were on either side of Thlayli, keeping him upright. The two women had burst into the room right after Young. There was a pause in which they had all looked at each other, before Phoebe rammed her horned head right into Young's back. There had been a crack, but the five of them didn't wait long. They had reached the elevator long before Young recovered.

"Phoebe, run to the car immediately. Tell Murphy to come here with Spot, she's big enough to carry Welei on her back." Josef's words were frantic. He could feel his voice draining out of him with every moment that passed. "Vanja and I will hold Young off as long as we can. Hurry!"

She ran out of the room before he was even done talking. Vanja was helping Thlayli rest against the statue of Sir Thaddeus in the centre of the room, while Josef threw himself at Phoebe's desk, hiding Welei there behind the solid wood. He noticed, out of the corner of his eye, that Vanja took a fire extinguisher to a water fountain, and he ran up to help her. He grasped the fountain with both hands, feeling the skin upon his back ripping. With a pull, the metal body of the fountain came away, and the water splashed across the floor. Vanja was muttering something in Croatian under her breath, her hands waving wildly over the spurting water. With a breathed-out curse, the water pressure increased, and the water shot up to the very ceiling.

Murphy had arrived in that moment, and Spot was leaving spots of sizzling, hot slobber in her wake. Phoebe was right behind him, her hand resting on his shoulder.

"Murphy, get Shark to the car. Phoebe, help Vanja get Thlayli to safety too." As he said that, he heard the elevator ding.

Young was a man of short stature, and yet it wasn't hard for him to seem intimidating. His bubbling, purulent face was enough to stop all of them in their tracks. His eyes were even brighter than before, and a steady flame of hatred burned within them. His hair had grown lighter, his face rounder. The gums inside his mouth were receding as he bared his teeth; his nose collapsed back into his face and his chin smoothed out.

"Filthy, thieving scum," he shrieked, moving towards them with jerking movements. "You use your uncle's name to get ahead in life, and now you insist on stealing my energy source too. Has anything you've ever done been your own idea, Josef? Have you ever done anything for yourself and not because some other person had the idea first? You're weak, Josef Brooke Ryan. Weak!"

Josef was aware that his hands were shaking. He was aware that the shiver was travelling up his arms and overcoming his torso, until his entire being was shaking. Maybe Young was right. Maybe he was just doing what everyone around him wanted him to do. He became an athlete for his mother, then turned to magizoology for Vanja. He studied hellhounds for Uncle Josef and dragons for his father, Dante. He had freed Welei and Thlayli because it was what they wanted, what they expected of him. He needed an entire ensemble of people to help him with the rescue. He wasn't even brave enough to visit his own father, not when Dante kept telling him he didn't have to.

"Brooke, don't listen to him! He lies, he's always lied to you!" Welei's voice cut through the silence that encroached upon him. Their face was peeking over the top of Phoebe's desk.

Everything happened so fast. Young launched himself at Welei, but Thlayli bodied him halfway to the desk. They fell, twisted around each other. Young's foot came down onto Thlayli's leg and a crunch followed. His hands wrapped around Thlayli's throat. A shrill, ear-piercing scream caused the windows to shiver, and Thlayli's teeth dug right into Young's cheek.

Vanja was by the statue of Sir Thaddeus, and the stream from the water fountain was shooting right at Young's back on her behest. He and Thlayli were right below the statue, flailing and writhing but refusing to let go of one another.

"Spot, get 'em!" Murphy's voice cut through the screaming. With a growl, a bark, and a whine, Spot lunged at Young. One of her heads grabbed him by the throat, another by the waist, and the third was snapping at his face as he attempted to keep her hot, slobbering maw away from him.

"Brooke, do something!" Phoebe and Murphy were with Thlayli; Welei was still behind the desk and Vanja was suddenly by them. Spot and Young were still by the statue. Josef approached it.

Josef pushed, and he could feel the muscles tear beneath his skin. He pushed, and he felt the burn on his back protest. He pushed, and the fire within his belly burned, feeding on his organs. He pushed, and his vision grew blurry, smoking billowing out of his nose with every pained huff.

There was nothing but the statue, the pain. The cacophony of screams was drowned out by his heartbeat drumming away in his ears. The light of the moon was but a pinprick, resting upon Young's struggling body. The statue was growing hot against his skin, Sir Thaddeus' handsome profile looking down at him with scorn. Young's mangled, and yet still beautiful, face was zeroed in on him with gnashing teeth, but Josef no longer saw him, nor the statue, nor anything but the blinding whiteness before his eyes. He just pushed.

He pushed for Shark who loved him despite his DNA. He pushed for Vanja who saw him as more than just the nephew of Josef Braun. He pushed for Phoebe and Murphy and Thlayli who saw him as a friend. He pushed for his father, Dante, who was always so proud of him. He pushed for his mother, Elspeth, who taught him to use his strength for good. He pushed for his Uncle Josef who taught him about his heritage. He pushed for his Uncle Brooke whose legacy had always been kindness and compassion. He pushed for himself, because he knew that he could, because he knew that he had to.

He pushed to prove Young wrong. He pushed to show Young that he was better. He pushed to show Young that he wasn't weak. He pushed and felt the rivulets of blood cascade down his back.

Josef Brooke Ryan pushed with a roar that echoed through the entire building, shattering the glass in every window. He pushed until the steel cords snapped and the statue tipped, teetered on the corner of its pedestal. Young barely had time to turn his head before it collapsed atop him. He didn't make a single sound. He simply smiled at Josef. And that smile reached his eyes.

Spot was at his side before his knees hit the linoleum floors. There was pain, a series of searing hot slashes across his back. The steel cords had left his skin shredded, the tension when they snapped shooting them backwards towards Josef and the statue. He felt as if his body had been filled up with acid that coursed through his veins, burning him from the inside. His hot blood burned; the lashes burned. He didn't even notice when his vision was going grey at the edges.

"Brooke, talk to me." The soft, melodic voice was paired with a delicate hand against his cheek. He couldn't place if that was Vanja or Welei.

"Talk to us, dragon-eyes." The familiar nickname had come from behind him, but he was in too much pain to turn his head.

"I'm alive," he whispered, his voice hoarse and his throat burning. When he swallowed, the fire within his lungs only worsened, scorching his throat further.

"You're alive, my love, you are." And this time Josef knew that it was Welei that was whispering into his ear, and it was their cheek that pressed against the side of his face.

He was alive, he was real, and the world hadn't ended after all.

16

—·—

SAYING GOODBYE

He woke up in the car when a pothole jostled him, and his entire back became bathed in ice. When the icy cold eased up, it burst into flames, and each small movement would interchange between cold, freezing pain, and a burning like that of the sun.

"Brooke, you're awake!" His hiss of pain had alerted Vanja, now in the driver's seat of Murphy's Kia. His vision was blurry, tears were streaming down his face, and yet he would've recognised her anywhere.

"Man, I'm so glad you're okay, Brooke." Murphy's voice was barely above a whisper, thick with sleep. He was pressed up against Josef's shoulder, and that was when Josef realised that Phoebe was the one in the passenger seat instead of him. His head hurt, pounding incessantly, and his back was tearing itself apart with every gentle jostle of the car.

His throat was thick, burning him as he tried to speak. "What happened?"

"The police arrived." Phoebe didn't elaborate, but she turned around in her seat, staring at him. Her earrings were dangling and catching glimpses of light that the moon outside cast upon the car. It was a welcome distraction from the pain.

"They miraculously let us take you away instead of calling an ambulance for you." Murphy's hand was outside of Josef's peripheral vision, and it hurt every time Josef tried turning his neck, but he was doing *something* with that hand. "Said that we'd take you there ourselves. But we're hoping your dad's nurse might be able to help out with that."

"Murphy turned into Young, and Phoebe helped him talk to police." Vanja's voice was also thick with sleepiness, and he had to wonder how long they had been driving, if they would make it, if all of this had been in vain or not. "We explained that statue of Sir Thaddeus fell and you got hurt."

"But ... what about Young? Couldn't they see his body?" His body, the body of a dead man, the body of Charles Young. By the ancestors, there was a body, there was a dead man. Josef had killed someone.

"There was nothing there, Brooke," Murphy mumbled into his shoulder. "Just dust." But dust that was once a body, was it not?

"You saved them, dragon-eyes."

He had killed a man. He was a murderer. Murphy's gentle hand grasped the back of his neck, ever so slightly moving his head until Josef was looking down. There was Spot laying across his feet, her three heads resting on the seat between him and Murphy. Then there were two rabbits, one doe-brown giant with lop ears, and one pitch black, skinny thing. They were curled up together in his lap, their tiny heads resting against his stomach.

"You saved them, Brooke."

He had saved them. These helpless, hurt beings who had been tormented by a cruel, inhuman man for years. They were safe because of him. He would have the scars to prove it, and the pain would forever be a reminder.

***

Sue met them at the door with a scream. Josef refused to have his back looked at. He rushed through the house, the others following behind.

"Are these your friends, hatchling?" Dante was uncomfortably pale, his skin taut over his face. He was cold to the touch when Josef reached out, and his eyes were completely white.

"Mhm. Vanja's here," Josef said, and he heard his voice as if on the other side of a tunnel. Dante's face lit up when his daughter came over to grasp his other hand.

"This is Murphy, my boyfriend." Vanja's voice was a whisper.

"This is Phoebe, my friend from work." Josef picked up from there. "That's Thlayli, with the long ears. And this ... this is Welei, my partner."

"Hi, dad," Welei said, hovering over Josef's shoulder, watching Dante smile. Their hand was pressed against Josef's elbow. They had eaten in the car and already seemed so light on their feet. Now they were there to catch him were he to fall.

"Oh, hatchling." Dante's voice grew weaker with every word. "I'm so happy for you. So, so happy." His warm breath created clouds of smoke before his face. The smoke eventually disappeared.

"He waited for us, Brooke," Vanja said. Her voice was barely there.

"He did. He held on for us, Vanja." Josef looked at her. They hugged. Over her shoulder he saw the last of the stars in the night sky blink out of existence.

***

In his will, Josef's father left him the cottage and another sum of money that he put away in a fund alongside the money his uncles left him. Over the coming days they settled in. Phoebe, Murphy, and Vanja left them after a week. Murphy had decided to 'inherit' the FCMC from his uncle, and Phoebe was ready to help him with all of the paperwork that entailed. No one had to know that Young was dead, they just had to think that he was bequeathing everything that he owned to his nephew and moving to an island somewhere to live out the rest of his days. Vanja had never been more on board with anything in her life, and Josef wasn't sure if he should have been worried about that.

That left Welei, Thlayli, and him. The cottage had been furnished in a rustic style Josef always had a soft spot for. There was a master bedroom he shared with Welei, and one of the guest bedrooms was given to Thlayli. Spot had her own mini-bedroom in the walk-in closet of the master bedroom. His father had thought of everything.

17

HEALING AFTER THE STORM

Healing was difficult. At least for him. Welei seemed to heal in such a short time that it was almost hard to believe.

"My love." Welei always talked to him when changing his bandages. The lacerations over his shoulders and arms had left him with permanent muscle damage, and the lashes that covered almost his entire back would ache until the day he died. And each day, as they peeled away the bloodied strips of cloth, careful not to cause any tearing, they whispered sweet nothings into his skin. Each day, as their lithe, alien hands worked and massaged a healing balm into his skin, they would hum and sing little songs they had heard on the radio or made up themself. Each day, as they rewound the bandages around his torso, tying the knot off into a perfect, little bow, they would call him 'love', and 'darling', and 'sweetheart', and 'my hero'. Josef liked that last one, he could hardly deny it. When the pain had his knees buckling, when it stopped him from falling asleep at night, 'my hero' made him remember why he had done it. When the amethyst eyes of Charles Young invaded his sleep, and the black sky outside pierced through his nightmares, 'my hero' kept him going. It was a decision he could hardly regret.

"*Mi tesoro*," he would mumble into the crown of Welei's head at night, the bags under his eyes heavy and dark, "I would kill for you again." It terrified him how much he meant it.

That was it, then, wasn't it? That was love. Over the coming months, they had made it from 'feeling' to 'love'. From simply a 'connection' to an intimacy they could never share with anyone else. But it wasn't at night when Josef loved them most. It wasn't in the throes of pleasure when Welei doted upon him, still bed-bound as he was. It wasn't in the bare-skinned hold they would have on each other, each time one of them woke up from a nightmare. Their nightmares often shared similarities, but it wasn't that which made Josef's heart burn, the dragon fire within his belly spreading out across his entire body until his whole being was engulfed with the overwhelming feeling of Welei.

It was in the day that he loved them most.

"I bought us chickens," they said one day, before Josef even had the time to notice they were gone all morning. Their hair was up in a long braid, and they were dressed in embroidered overalls, carrying a pair of chickens, one under each arm. He was sitting at the kitchen table with his glasses discarded (he never wore them around the cottage), shirtless and without any bandages, as the cloth tended to make his fresh scars itch.

"Weren't you supposed to be in bed, Shark?"

Welei let out a melodic giggle at the nickname, flashing Josef their shark-like teeth. Their lips pressed against his brow, and one of the chickens let out a loud cluck in protest.

"I was, but I felt bored. Vanja said she'd meet me at the farmer's market in the nearby town." They were beaming as they set the chickens down in the middle of the kitchen, cooing at the birds and listening to them cluck. Josef almost regretted getting them a mobile phone, until he noticed the healthy flush upon their cheeks and the way their face was rounding out with every day that passed. Their skin no longer looked translucent and was even tanning gently from all the time they spent in the garden. He might have still been semi-bed-bound, but Vanja was giving them a run for their money. And they loved it. Moments like these reminded Josef of why he loved them so much.

The daytime love eventually bled into their nightly activities. When he lay in bed with them at night, their arms no longer felt fragile wrapped around his neck, their body no longer promising to slip from his fingers like smoke. Their body was still cold to the touch, but he made up for it with the fire that burned in his belly. They didn't need intimacy anymore to love each other, they didn't need bodies to show one another that they mattered. Not when the sun rose in the morning and made Welei's skin glow in a way that took Josef's breath away, or when the stars peppered the night sky and Welei could see their own galaxy reflected in Josef's russet eyes.

Love was a feeling, but very few feelings truly compared to love.

"What if we bought a goat?" Josef reached out and pressed a finger against Welei's cheek. They let out a snort that was just as melodic as the rest of their laughs, even if it made them sound like a little piggy.

"Really? You mean that? Brookie, I love you!"

"I love you too." And that was the easiest thing Josef had ever done: chosen to love Welei with his whole heart.

***

Thlayli mostly stayed up in his room during the months he was healing. Three times a day Welei would bring food up to him, juggling the responsibility of helping him and helping Josef. Maybe it was because they were an alien that they never seemed to run out of energy.

Thlayli didn't need his bandages changed like Josef did, but his broken leg healed slowly, aggravated by the shifts he was forced into during the night. Welei tried, on multiple occasions, to bring him and Josef together into one room, to let them recuperate together. In the early days the pain made Josef loopy, barely conscious of anything that was going on around him. Thlayli simply preferred being alone.

However, when he was able to, he would do exercises. Welei would pull him up and off the bed, slowly walking around the room with him. He would let out silent whimpers in the first few months, scrunching his face up with pain. And yet he kept at it, and soon was able to walk on his own again. Soon, he was walking to the master bedroom with little steps. He would sit with Welei, watching them go through exercises with Josef, getting some movement into the muscles of his massacred back.

"I'll never move my arms normally again," Josef would often bemoan, regurgitating the hurried words of the nurse, Sue. Thlayli would scooch up to him, dislodging Welei from their spot. He would press his cold nose against Josef's side and watch with glee as his arms flailed wildly.

"I dunno," Welei would respond with merriment, "you're doing great, if you ask me." That was in the later months, however, of their healing.

In the early days, when unable to move from the bed, Thlayli loved reading or being read to. He had a copy of *Watership Down* on his bedside table and would force Welei, and later Josef as well, to read it to him. Welei knew it off by heart by the time Thlayli first ended up with Young but would still indulge him by pretending to read off the page. Welei couldn't count the amount of times Thlayli had fallen asleep on their shoulder as they read to him. They could only hope he dreamt of his own Watership Down.

In the later days, Thlayli would often visit Josef when Welei was away. They would sit together for an hour at a time, Josef teaching him hand signs. First finger spelling, then simple words like 'eat', 'drink', or 'sleep'. By the end of his stay, they were having entire conversations. Josef, bed-bound as he was, thought the world of Thlayli whenever he came over to his room to visit. Thlayli, once he knew how, would not stop thanking Josef for indulging him. Welei would often watch on as they signed back and forth, simply smiling.

Their conversations eventually led to Thlayli asking to go home.

--·--

INTERLUDE 5: JOSEF, WELEI, AND THLAYLI

They were standing at the edge of the forest, a few miles from the Ryan-Braun cottage. Shark watched as Thlayli undressed, handing each article of clothing to Josef. He stood there for a few heart beats, his short fur standing on end from the light breeze. The shift took but a few seconds, preceded by him bringing his hand up to his face. With a flat palm pressed against the tip of his chin, he moved his hand in an arc away from himself. Then, once he was back to his rabbit form, he disappeared into the brush.

Josef took a step back, moving into Welei's awaiting arms. He was shaking, not from the cold but from something else.

"Are you sure this is right?" Josef watched Thlayli disappear beneath the protection of the trees. Welei smiled at him, bringing their face closer to his neck, soaking up his warmth.

"It's what he wants, Brooke," Welei whispered against his collarbone, their wide, endless eyes tracing the path Thlayli took through the underbrush. "He'll be back. No matter how many times he told me he wouldn't return, he always did. We'll see him again."

"And when we do," Josef added, his voice growing thick, "he'll be happy again."

"He will, my love. He will. And so will we."

ABOUT THE AUTHOR

Booker-Garet August Feniks (known under the penname Booker G. A Feniks) is a queer, disabled writer of fantasy, comedy, & poetry. He writes stories that pull directly from their experiences growing up trans & autistic in a foreign country. Originally from Poland, Kielce, Booker writes primarily in English, & has a passion for linguistics & storytelling as a whole. He is young, ambitious, & optimistic about the changing future, although not unfamiliar with activism & the more difficult aspects of growing up marginalised.

— · —

BEFORE YOU GO

This is the third book in 12 Months of Whump, a series of whumpy novellas published by WPP throughout 2025. Each novella can be read as a standalone.
To stay up to date with the 12 Months of Whump series and other whumperfly-inducing projects, visit us at https://thewhumpyprintingpress.tumblr.com/